Magical Moon Cat

Jax could see Howard at the bottom of the
garden, peering around in some bushes.
"Howard!" she called. "It's me, Jax!"

In her hurry to tell him the good news
she almost tripped over an enormous red box
that someone had left in the middle of the
grass. On the box, in glittery writing, it said:
MISTER MAGICK. Everything the young
magician needs to get started...

Magical Moon Cat

Moonbeans and the Talent Show

Annie Dalton

USBORNE

For Kara, Cora, Niamh and their friends

First published in 2012 by Usborne Publishing Ltd., Usborne House, 83-85 Saffron Hill, London EC1N 8RT, England. www.usborne.com

Text copyright © Annie Dalton, 2012 Cover illustration by Tuesday Mourning. Inside illustrations by Katie Lovell. Illustration copyright © Usborne Publishing Ltd, 2012

The name Usborne and the devices ♀ 🎈 are Trade Marks of Usborne Publishing Ltd.

A CIP catalogue record for this book is available from the British Library.

ISBN 9781409526339 02590/1
JFMAM JASOND/12

Printed in Dongguan, Guangdong China.

Contents

Cosmic cupcakes

1

It was a muggy midsummer's day and Jax was having more trouble than usual staying awake in morning assembly.

She could see her friend Lilia fighting a yawn, which set her off yawning too. On the other side of Jax, Howard was also having trouble staying awake, sitting with his head bowed almost to the floor, his long floppy hair falling across his face like a curtain. Howard was the strangest, and also the quietest, boy Jax had ever met. In class, he wrote brilliant, rather weird, stories, but hardly ever spoke unless their teacher asked him a direct question. In the playground, he just mooched around by himself.

Jax sneaked a look at her watch and closed her eyes in despair. *Six* hours until home time! Six whole hours before she could sit under the twisty old lilac tree behind her mum's café, talking to Moonbeans, her magical moon cat.

She quickly opened her eyes. She had promised herself she wouldn't daydream about Beans. Real life and magic had to be kept separate – Jax had learned that the hard way. But how could you NOT think about an alien kitten who was also your best friend? It was impossible!

She suddenly felt Lilia poking her in the

ribs. "My mum's invented some new cupcakes for your mum's café!" Lilia whispered from behind her hand. "She calls them 'cosmic cupcakes'! They actually explode!"

The thought of cosmic cupcakes, especially exploding ones, instantly perked Jax up. Lilia's mum, Nadia, made all the cakes and pastries for Jax's mum's café. This meant that Jax and Lilia were usually the first people to sample Nadia's amazing creations.

"Mum gave me two to bring in for us to try," Lilia said in a hoarse whisper.

"Can I see them?" Jax whispered back.

"Of course not, silly!" Lilia rolled her eyes. "You've got to wait till break for the big reveal!"

Jax snickered. "You watch too much telly, Lilia!"

"Ssh!" Mrs. Chaudhary, their teacher, gave them a sharp look. "*No talking*," she mouthed.

There was a sudden rustling from the stage as Mr. Tattersall, the headmaster, folded up his sheet of paper. He had finished the week's announcements. Breathing a sigh of relief, Jax got ready for him to tell everyone to return to their classrooms. Instead, he beamed around at them all. "I have one final and very special announcement," he said.

She muffled a groan. Not *another* announcement!

"You have all worked extremely hard this term," he told them, still beaming. "So your teachers and I decided that you deserve a reward. Goose Green Primary School is going to put on its first ever talent show!"

Everybody gasped. Well, almost everybody; Howard didn't gasp, but Jax felt him go super-still behind his hair, as if he was genuinely fascinated to know what Mr. Tattersall was

10

going to say next. Jax thought this was surprising. Talent shows were about showing off in public – why would this super-shy boy be interested in showing off?

There was a buzz of excitement as everyone took in the news. Ruby-Rose and Conrad started whispering with their heads together. Conrad had used too much hair gel this morning, Jax thought with a grin. His ginger spikes looked even stiffer and perkier than normal.

Mr. Tattersall had to clap his hands to restore order. Everyone hushed at once. Only Conrad carried on enthusiastically chatting, until Ruby-Rose hissed at him to stop. He suddenly noticed everyone looking at him and broke into a grin. "Sorry, sir! Don't mind me, sir! I got a bit overexcited!"

Everyone burst out laughing. Mr. Tattersall had to wait for their giggles to die down before he could finish explaining about the talent show. "The show will be held in the last week of term. That's only three weeks away," he reminded them. "So if any of you think you've got a special talent, if you can sing, dance, juggle or do impressions, and you'd like to perform in the show, give your name to Mrs. Pearl, the school secretary. And then you'd better start rehearsing!" He gave them another warm smile. "Now make your way back to your classrooms – and remember, WALK, don't run!"

At morning break, Jax waited impatiently for Lilia to produce her exploding cosmic cupcakes, but her friend just wanted to talk about the talent show.

"What shall we do for our act?" Lilia asked.

"I'm not going to enter," Jax told her.

"Oh!" Lilia sulked. "Why not?"

"For one thing, I don't have a talent!"

"You do!" Lilia objected. "You do karate. We could do that cool routine we did at Ruby-Rose's party."

"I don't want to be in it, Lilia," Jax said firmly. Ever since Moonbeans's spaceship had crashed to Earth in her back garden, Jax had been secretly helping him with a very special mission: making Goose Green a happier place for all the life forms that lived there. Which meant she *really* didn't have time for things like talent contests. "You can still enter though," she pointed out.

Lilia looked horrified. "I couldn't get up onstage all by myself!"

"Why don't you find someone who wants to be in the show like you and do something with them?" Jax suggested.

"But I want to do it with *you!*" Lilia wailed.

Jax sighed to herself. That was the thing about Lilia – she had this idea that best friends always had to do everything together. "Lilia, I wouldn't be any good," she pointed out. "You'd honestly be much better teaming up with someone who's as mad keen to do it as you are. If you really want to be in the show, someone perfect will turn up," Jax reassured her. Then she went tingly all over because that was like something Moonbeans would say. Maybe his

 moon magic was starting to rub off on her?

"Hello, girls!" Conrad's freckled face was one big grin as he ran up to join them. "Guess what I'm doing in the talent show!"

"A mushy love duet," Lilia suggested, giggling.

Conrad pretended to choke himself. "No way, José!" he said in disgust. "Go on, Jax, have a guess!"

Jax laughed. "I have no idea, but knowing you it will be mad and fun!"

"Got it in one, Jackson," he said with a grin. "I'm doing street dance! Ruby-Rose says she'll help me with my moves. She thinks I'm brilliant!"

"I didn't say you were brilliant, Conrad! I said you had your own very special style!"

Ruby-Rose had come up behind him.

Conrad didn't even blink. "That's what I said! Special, stylish and brilliant!" he said smugly. "Actually, Ruby, you might want to do your act first. Anyone who comes on after me is going to be a real let-down – know what I'm saying?"

Ruby-Rose just laughed and tweaked one of his spikes.

"Are you entering the talent show, Ruby?" Jax had assumed that Ruby-Rose would never want to perform again now she'd given up being a child star.

Ruby-Rose nodded. "I'm going to recite a really cool cat poem I used to do for auditions."

Excellent choice, Jax thought. If it wasn't for a certain little alien cat and his magical missions, Ruby-Rose's mum would still be dragging her off to endless auditions.

Ruby-Rose was *much* nicer to be around now she was just a normal person, and it was all thanks to Moonbeans – and his human sidekick, Jax, aka Ellie Mae Jackson, she thought, hiding her smile. Then she realized she was thinking about magic again, and gave herself a brisk little shake.

She could hear Meena and Pritty telling everyone that they'd signed up to perform their mirror dance. A few metres away, Bella and Jasmine were trying to persuade Keisha and Ebony to form a girl band. It seemed like everybody suddenly wanted to show off their special talents.

Jax could see Howard mooching by himself over by the wall. She couldn't see his expression because of his hair, but she could feel him listening intently to everyone's conversations.

Eventually Lilia was persuaded to move to a quieter part of the playground, and Jax got to see the famous cosmic cupcakes. Jax stared down into the Tupperware box. "Wow!" she breathed. "They do look *really* cosmic!" Nadia had iced each cake with sparkly midnight blue icing and topped them with a pattern of shooting stars. "Do they seriously explode?" she asked with interest.

Lilia nodded. "They seriously do! They've got a surprise ingredient."

"It's not dangerous, is it?" Jax said nervously.

"No, silly. It's space dust! Not *real* space dust obviously!" Lilia said, giggling. "It's this harmless chemical that explodes in your mouth. Try one!"

Jax didn't need telling twice! She took a greedy bite and immediately started munching. Lilia burst out laughing at her expression as teeny explosions went off inside Jax's mouth. She quickly swallowed her mouthful. "I *like* it!" she beamed, and took another huge bite.

The Aunts will LOVE hearing about these, Jax thought with a grin, as the space dust popped and crackled inside her mouth. "The Aunts" was what Beans called the wise and mysterious beings who had sent him on his first ever mission to Earth. Beans said they were totally ancient, even older than the stars, and they'd been watching over this planet for centuries. The Aunts were fascinated by everything to do with Planet Earth, so Jax had got in the habit of looking out for things for Moonbeans to tell them when he spoke to them.

She pictured herself under the lilac tree,

telling him about the exploding cupcakes and the talent show. The thought made her smile…

"You're happy all of a sudden," said Lilia at once.

"I am so happy I could burst!" Jax said truthfully. She had just sneaked a look at her watch. In four hours, school would be finished. She'd have a whole weekend with Moonbeans.

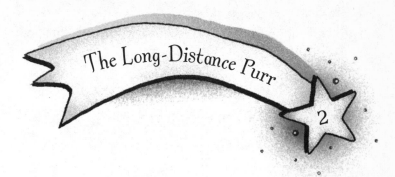

The Long-Distance Purr

2

The first time Jax had set eyes on Dolly's Diner, which was what her mum's café was originally called, she'd thought it was the most depressing building she had ever seen! There were mice running around in the storeroom and the walls were covered with grease. Mum was constantly having mad ideas, but Jax had been sure that taking over this run-down old café was her worst idea ever!

It turned out Jax was wrong. In just a few short months, Mum's café had become a runaway success and was now the most popular café in Goose Green. Jax knew her mum had worked hard to get it up and running, but she also knew that she never would have pulled it off without a little magical help from Moonbeans – and the Aunts of course. They had wanted Mum's café to become a magical meeting place – a place where dreams could come true. And that was exactly what had happened.

Even the café's freshly painted sign with its new name, The Dream Café, in rainbow letters that shimmered like moonlight, was down to Beans. Tired, hungry shoppers noticed the eye-catching sign, then they caught a wonderful whiff of good coffee and the scent of freshly baked cakes and pastries, and they *had* to go in. They couldn't help themselves.

When Mum's customers talked about the new café, they usually mentioned its friendly vibe. They rarely mentioned the marmalade kitten that sometimes weaved around their ankles, purring with an unusually intense purr.

He's doing it again, Jax thought, as she walked through the door that afternoon after school. She grinned to herself as she watched the little moon kitten go trotting up to a harassed mother who was trying to soothe her two grizzling toddlers.

If Jax didn't know better she would think he was just a normal kitten with golden eyes slightly too big for his cute little face. But Jax did know better. Beans closed his eyes and Jax could tell he was doing one of his Purrs of Power. She saw the woman's frazzled expression turn into a smile. Her toddlers stopped grizzling, and held out their chubby little hands to the cute kitty. Jax smiled to herself. She called this "The Moonbeans effect". Customers came in looking stressed, and left looking as if they'd had a fortnight's holiday.

Jax looked around for her mum and spotted her by the display cabinet, carefully removing cupcakes with a pair of tongs.

"Hi, Mum," she said cheerfully.

"Hi, Ellie Mae!" said her mum, sliding the cupcakes onto a plate.

Jax rolled her eyes. She was always telling her mum to just call her "Jax", but she took no notice. "When I'm grown up, I'm officially going to change my name – then you'll *have* to call me 'Jax'," she told her now.

"Don't bank on it," Mum said cheerfully.

"You're not going to win this one, Mum." Jax

helped herself to a bottle of
fizzy pink lemonade from the
cooler cabinet.

"Oh yes I am!" her mum
sang back.

Jax felt something soft brush
against her ankles and immediately crouched
down to stroke her little cat. "Beans!"

Jax always thought it was strange that she
was the only person to notice the magical
sparkles in his fur. Maybe it was because she
was the only person who knew her little cat's
true identity. Moonbeans wasn't from our
world. He wasn't even from our solar system.
He was a moon cat from a totally unknown
planet millions of light years away from Earth.
No wonder she found it hard to concentrate at
school, Jax thought as she lovingly scratched
him between the ears. No wonder she was

always counting the minutes till she could race back to the Dream Café and hang out with her cute little alien cat.

"I see you've been a busy bee while I've been away!" she teased him.

How can you tell? Beans seemed surprised.

"Are you kidding?" she said with a grin. "The entire café is as fizzy as this pink lemonade!" From the start, Jax and Beans had been able to read each other's minds. Beans could read hers because that was how moon cats communicated, and Jax could read his mind because she was his special human. "Let's go in the garden," she added in a low voice, "it'll be cooler out there."

Jax and Beans hurried out through a side door into the café's tiny back garden. Using her school cardigan for a picnic blanket, Jax threw herself down under the twisty old lilac tree, just as she'd been picturing all through her long day at school. Beans lay down beside her and lazily started to wash.

"It's so stuffy today!" Jax unscrewed the cap from her bottle of lemonade and had a thirsty gulp.

There's going to be a storm. Beans's ears twitched as he sniffed the air.

Jax started telling him about her day. Beans was fascinated by the idea of exploding cosmic cupcakes and immediately wanted to try one, but he seemed puzzled when she told him about the school talent show.

Is it the same as a concert?

"Kind of – except people don't just sing or dance or play musical instruments," she explained. "They do all kinds of other things,

like juggling and
acrobatics. There's
this girl, Bonnie,
who is going to play
Puff the Magic Dragon
on water glasses!"

Jax had started to stroke her kitten,
breathing in the other-worldly smell that still
clung to his fur. The smell always reminded her
of jelly beans, which was why she'd named him
"Moonbeans".

"Beans," she said suddenly, "when do you
think we'll get our next mission? It's been ages
now."

I'm not sure, but I think it could be really soon!

"Me too!" she said eagerly. She was gently
brushing his fur the wrong way, revealing the
shimmery tiger stripes hidden underneath.
Beans had told her that his stripes were hidden

because he was only half moon cat. Beans's magical mum had met his Earth-cat dad when she was visiting our planet with a secret moon-cat delegation. Jax had never told Beans, but she loved that he was half Earth cat. It made him seem more like hers.

Beans seemed unusually quiet and thoughtful. Jax suddenly remembered that she hadn't asked him about his day and worried that he might be offended. "So what have you been up to?" she asked, kissing his nose. "You haven't been meeting and greeting Mum's customers *all* day, surely?"

I've been looking for Rumble, he said.

"Whatever for?" Jax said rudely, before she could stop herself. Mum was always telling her to think twice before she opened her mouth.

Because he's my friend, Beans said with dignity, *and I'm worried about him.*

Rumble was a stinky
old tomcat who roamed
around the streets
of Goose Green.
Moonbeans was
genuinely fond of Rumble,
not seeming to mind the strong pong of stale
fish that followed him everywhere he went.
According to Beans, Rumble knew all about
moon cats paying visits to our planet and had
been patiently waiting for Moonbeans to show
up in Goose Green.

Jax knew that Beans really trusted Rumble
because he'd asked the old warrior cat to help
him find his dad. Rumble had promised to put
the word out on the street. But so far nothing
had happened.

"So why are you so worried about Rumble
all of a sudden?" Jax was just asking to be

polite, not because she actually wanted to know.

No one's seen him for days, Beans explained.
*I've been to all his usual places but there's no sign
of him anywhere.*

"I'm sure he'll turn up," Jax said. "He's
probably got shut in somewhere."

Maybe. But Jax could tell Beans wasn't
convinced.

That night Jax woke to hear thunder rumbling
around the rooftops. The air felt unpleasantly
sticky and she could hear a group of teenagers
messing around down in the street. But it wasn't
the thunder or the teenagers that had woken
her. Beans was doing a very special Purr of
Power.

He was sitting by her window, his tail curled
around his paws, and his eyes fixed on a faintly
twinkling far-off star as he purred. Jax had seen

him do this before, so she knew that the star was just to help him focus. The vibrations of his purr were actually travelling right past the star, across the Milky Way and beyond, to a strange little planet that none of Earth's scientists had ever seen. This must be Beans's night for reporting back to the Aunts.

All Beans's Purrs of Power made Jax go fizzy inside, but his Long-Distance Purr made Jax *seriously* buzzy. As Beans purred and purred, everything around him started to glow with a rosy pink light. The buzzing sensation in Jax's tummy grew stronger as the light started to flicker and flash, lighting up random corners of her room. *Flash!* There was her precious telescope that had belonged to her dad. *Flash!* Now it was her bookshelf crammed with books about space. *Flash!* This time it was her goldfish, Brad, swimming excitedly up and down in his tank.

It had been a sticky night to begin with. Now, with so much magic in the air, Jax was getting uncomfortably hot, so she climbed on top of her quilt to cool down. It was pointless trying to go back to sleep while her room was jumping with magic vibes, so she just hugged her knees, and waited for Beans to finish. Conversations between Beans and the Aunts usually took a while, but you wouldn't hear Jax complain. If it wasn't for the Aunts, she and Beans would never have met. Somehow, these kindly beings had known that the nine-year-old human girl and the little moon cat belonged together.

As she listened to the steady rhythm of Beans's purr ebbing and flowing, Jax found herself remembering the day it all began. She had been so lonely when she first arrived in Goose Green. She missed her grandpa, who they'd left behind on the other side of the city. She missed her friends. And she still really missed her dad, who had died when she was six years old. Her dad had been a scientist, fascinated by anything to do with stars and planets and space. Because of him, Jax had grown to love them too.

It was because of her dad that she had secretly dreamed of meeting an alien, ever since he'd explained that the word simply meant "stranger", someone you didn't know yet. So when an alien actually landed in her back garden for real, she wasn't scared like most humans would be. She was thrilled to pieces because her dream was finally coming true.

But Moonbeans had never seemed like a stranger, she thought, hugging her knees. He was like the best friend she had been longing for all her life. With a magical moon cat for company, Jax knew she'd never feel lonely again.

Jax suddenly noticed that the purring had stopped. There was a light thud as Moonbeans jumped down from the window. He'd finally finished his long-distance call. Outside, the storm had broken and Jax could hear the first raindrops hitting her window.

Moonbeans sprang up onto her bed. *You're awake!* He seemed surprised.

"You try sleeping through the Amazing Space-Travelling Purr, mister!" she said, swallowing a yawn. "So how is everyone doing on the little planet with five moons?" The fact that it had five moons was one of the few things Jax knew about Beans's planet.

The Aunts sent their love.

"They must have said more than that," Jax objected. "You were chatting for hours."

They wanted to know what midsummer is like in Goose Green.

"Noisy!" said Jax.

I told them there was music coming out of all the cars. They wanted to know what kind of music.

"All kinds!" Jax said with a grin. It really tickled her how things that seemed so ordinary to her were totally exotic to the Aunts.

Moonbeans gracefully collapsed beside Jax and started to wash. "Aren't you going to tell me what they said?" she prompted him.

It's late. You should be sleeping.

"I *was* sleeping, actually, Beans! You woke me up! Anyway it's Friday night, which means no school tomorrow and I want to know what they said. Did the Aunts say it's time?"

Beans looked blank. *Time?*

"For our next mission," she said.

Moonbeans went back to washing, making loud buzzing sounds in his fur. He was teasing her, she realized. "*Beans!* Tell me what they said or I'll throw this pillow at you. Is it time or isn't it?"

Beans looked up and blinked his amber gold eyes. *It's time.*

"YAY!" Jax cheered, then remembered it was the middle of the night. *"Yay!"* she said again in a whisper. "I wonder who we'll have to help this time?"

Who or possibly *what*? Beans constantly reminded Jax that his mission was to help *all* the life forms of Goose Green live happier lives, not just humans. *I really hope it isn't a slug,* she thought with a shudder.

We have to be asked, remember? Beans said. *The Aunts only tell us when it's time.*

"I want to know who it is *now*!" she moaned. "I won't sleep a wink."

Yes, you will, Beans said firmly.

Jax bashed at her pillows. "I won't! I don't ever sleep when you do that Long-Distance Purr. It makes me too buzzy."

Beans fitted himself into the crook of her arm and began to do what Jax called his "lullaby purr" – a soothing sound that travelled all the way from the roots of her hair to the soles of her feet, smoothing out all the parts of Jax that felt too fizzy. A sudden yawn took her by surprise.

"I do love you, Beans," she said sleepily. "I'm so glad the Aunts picked me to be your huma—" But she fell asleep before she could finish her sentence.

The opposite of cute

3

When morning came, Jax didn't need to open her eyes to know that the rain had stopped – she could feel bright sunlight flickering on and off her eyelashes.

In a flash, she had her day planned out. On sunny Saturdays, Mum was always madly busy in the café; it was the perfect opportunity to hang out in the garden with Moonbeans. But when she sat up in bed, he wasn't there!

A dreamlike memory floated back. It had been almost light and birds were twittering in the rain-drenched gardens behind the café. *I've*

got to find Rumble,
Beans had told
her urgently. *I*
think he's in real
trouble. He'd
slipped out
through her open

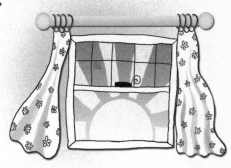

window into the dawn and Jax had immediately
gone back to sleep.

Remembering this conversation now, Jax let
out a groan. Obviously she didn't want Rumble
to come to any harm, but if he was their new
assignment, she was not impressed!

Jax and Beans's first mission had been to
help Mum make her dream café into a real-life
success. Their second was to help Ruby-Rose
realize that trying to make her mum happy, by
being a child star, was making Ruby-Rose *really*
*un*happy! Jax had hoped to be rewarded for

their good deeds with a thrilling new mission, and what did they get? A smelly old tomcat!

"Couldn't we at least help someone cute?" Jax grumbled to her goldfish. "Rumble has to be, like, the total *opposite* of cute."

She stomped over to her window to see if she could see Beans in any of the gardens.

But she could only see Howard. His house was part of a square of tall, grand-looking houses with long back gardens. He was outside in his pyjamas, carrying his giant pet rabbit draped over his shoulder like a fluffy white blanket. He was too far away for her to be able to see his face but she thought he looked lonely.

Watching Howard mooch about in his dripping wet garden, Jax remembered how she used to feel jealous because he had a pet. Then Moonbeans came and now she wouldn't change places with shy, lonely Howard for anything. *I'm so lucky*, she thought, and she felt a twinge of guilt for sulking about Rumble. So what if a stinky old cat wasn't her ideal life form? He was one of Beans's best friends. She could at least try to be kind.

Moonbeans reappeared while she was having breakfast. He had a cobweb hanging off one of his whiskers and smelled unusually musty. *Come quickly*, he told her. *I've found Rumble but there's something wrong with him. He's in the shed.*

That must be where he'd picked up the cobweb, Jax thought. She scraped back her chair. "It's such a lovely day," she told her mum brightly. "I think I'll go in the garden with Beans!"

In the days of Dolly's Diner, the back garden had been a depressing little yard where they'd kept the bins. Jax's mum had transformed it with pots of flowers and herbs, painting the 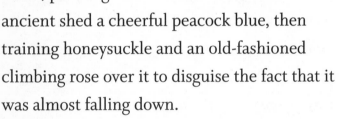 ancient shed a cheerful peacock blue, then training honeysuckle and an old-fashioned climbing rose over it to disguise the fact that it was almost falling down.

Bees were humming in the roses as Jax peeped cautiously around the shed door. Rumble was crouching on a pile of yellowing newspapers, making harsh wheezing sounds as if it hurt to breathe.

This was a different Rumble to the tough warrior cat Jax had seen swaggering around Goose Green, keeping the local cats in line. But it turned out there was still a bit of fight left in him. When he saw Jax, his ears went flat and he gave a low growl of warning.

Rumble doesn't like humans, Beans said.

No kidding! Jax thought. Rumble had looked bigger out of doors, she thought. In the musty gloom of the shed, he seemed pathetically bony, plus there was some weird gummy stuff coming out of his eyes that made Jax quickly look away. "How did you know he needed help anyway?" She was keeping her voice down so as not to alarm the poorly Rumble.

I saw him in my dream, Beans explained. *He was out in the rain, getting splashed by the traffic, so I went to get him.* He gave his friend a quick lick on one of his tattered ears, and when

Rumble didn't protest, settled down to give him a proper wash. *He'll feel better when he's clean*, Beans explained and he began to purr. Jax thought it sounded almost, but not exactly, like his late-night lullaby purr.

As she watched her little moon cat patiently washing Rumble's bedraggled fur, Jax felt a pang of worry. Rumble did look really poorly. "I'm going to get my mum," she said abruptly. Purring and washing was all very well but Jax thought what Rumble needed was a vet.

 It was time for the café to open. Lexie, their new Saturday girl, was taking down the shutters. Jax's mum was talking to Nadia, who had just brought a fresh delivery of cupcakes. Mum looked up in surprise as Jax burst in. "Sweetie, what's wrong?"

"Our shed door was open so I went to close it," Jax said breathlessly. "And I saw Rumble inside, huddled up on some newspapers." She'd decided not to mention Beans's part in all of this.

Her mum frowned. "You don't mean that old homeless cat Beans hangs around with?"

"Mum, he's *really* poorly. Please, you've got to come." Jax was practically hopping from foot to foot.

"Do you mind hanging on here for a few minutes?" Mum asked Nadia with a sigh. "I'll just be a minute."

Moments later, Mum was standing just inside the shed door, clutching her inhaler. Moonbeans was the only cat on Planet Earth that didn't bring on Mum's allergies. Jax and Beans thought this was probably because he came from a different planet.

Rumble had made himself a little lair behind some boxes. Jax could just see angry yellow-green eyes glaring out of the shadows. Beans was perching on one of the boxes, obviously watching over his friend. He was still purring in a steady hypnotic rhythm, and Jax thought the dark little shed looked suspiciously fizzy. She found it hard to believe her mum hadn't noticed, even though Beans had told Jax that most humans stopped believing in magic once they started school. This hadn't happened to Jax luckily and she was fiercely determined that it never would. Jax had believed in magic her whole life and she intended to go on believing in it for ever and ever.

Mum had edged forward to get a closer look. She made a sympathetic *tsk*ing sound. "Poor old boy. He has been in the wars. I'd better phone Cat Rescue."

Jax was horrified. "No way, Mum!" People went to Cat Rescue to get a cute kitten. Nobody wanted to adopt a smelly old fighter cat.

Mum took a puff from her inhaler. "We can't just leave him here and hope for the best," she objected.

"I know. That's why I came to get you. Rumble needs a vet."

Her mum was screwing up her face waiting for a sneeze. "Ellie, you are a kind girl, but vets cost a lot of – ASHOO! – money."

Quick, Moonbeans, help! Jax begged silently. Beans's soothing purr immediately switched to a more urgent sound.

Yay! Jax gave a silent cheer. Beans was doing the Purr of Power!

The shed had been pink and fizzy before.

49

Now it began to pulse with a brilliant pink glow. Jax could see a struggle going on inside her mum, then her expression softened. "You know what, Ellie Mae? I think you're right. We ought to call the vet."

Jax threw her arms around her mum. "Thanks, Mum."

"That's assuming we can find a vet who does house calls. I can't see Rumble being too happy to jump in my car!" Mum ruffled Jax's hair. "Now can I please get on with running my café?" she joked.

The boy in the purple cloak

4

After lunch, Jax went to check on Rumble. The minute she walked in the shed she could hear him wheezing painfully inside his cardboard box fortress, his bony ribs moving up and down with every rattling breath. Nadia had given Mum the number of a friendly vet she knew who did house calls. Mum had rung her and she'd promised to call in later that afternoon. Jax *really* hoped she didn't leave it too long, because things didn't look too good for poor old Rumble. She'd done everything she could think of to make him comfortable. She'd given him some clean water, and now she'd brought mashed sardines in an old saucer to tempt him. There was nothing she could do except wait. Closing the shed door softly behind her, she left him to sleep.

Jax was thirsty now, so she ran to fetch a cool drink from the café and came back to join Beans, who was sunning himself in the garden, with three tiny white butterflies for company.

She sat down beside him, kicking off her new flip-flops to let the sun get to her toes. The flip-flops were a present from her grandpa. It was funny how he kept sending her little presents, yet he never came to visit. She gave a wistful sigh.

You miss your grandpa, don't you?

Jax was used to Beans reading her mind. She

gave a forlorn nod. "Before we moved to Goose Green I saw him every day. My mum misses him too. But she says she doesn't want to be the one who always phones."

He came to your mum's launch, Beans remembered.

Jax was picking daisies to make a daisy chain. "The thing is, I don't know *why* he came. I don't know if it was because I left a message or because you did that moon magic. Mum's asked him to come and stay loads of times, but he always finds some exc—" Jax broke off mid-sentence. She stared up at the sky with a wondering expression. Crowds of rose-pink sparkles were floating down through the air. She held out her hand to catch one. It shimmered there like a snowflake, then

 vanished, leaving her skin feeling tingly. "Beans!" she said urgently. "Are these sparkles, like, a *message* from the Aunts?"

How did you know? Beans seemed impressed.

"Because they sent them before we got our mission to help Ruby-Rose. But we've got a mission already – we're looking after Rumble. So why are the Aunts sending sparkles now?"

Moonbeans looked startled. *Rumble isn't our mission. Why did you think he was our mission?*

Jax was totally confused. "I – I just sort of assumed," she stammered. "You're sure he isn't our mission?"

We have to be asked, remember? Rumble never asks anyone for anything.

"Oh, wow, so we're still waiting to find out who we've got to help?" Jax didn't want to say this aloud, but maybe now they'd get someone exciting!

She was quiet for a few minutes as she concentrated on finishing her daisy chain. Finally she joined on the last daisy. "This is for you, Beans. Stay still and I'll put it on."

She was just slipping the fragile daisy collar around his neck when she saw a flash of white as a huge white rabbit came lolloping through a gap in the hedge.

Jax's eyes went wide. She looked around at the pink sparkles and the tiny white butterflies and the little moon cat wearing a daisy chain; then she looked back at the rabbit. "Beans?" she whispered. "Is that rabbit real?"

Don't you recognize him? That's Howard's rabbit. Beans seemed amused.

Jax puffed out her cheeks with relief. She had forgotten about Howard's pet rabbit. For a minute, she'd been afraid this was all just a dream!

When the rabbit saw Jax and Beans, he froze, nervously whiffling his nose as if he was deciding whether to bolt back the way he'd come. Then, reaching up a snowy white paw, he pulled down one of his long white ears and gave it a quick wash.

Jax slipped her feet back into her flip-flops. "I'll go and tell Howard his rabbit's escaped." She ran into the café to tell her mum what had happened.

Mum laughed. "First it's a stray cat, now it's a rabbit. What will you find in our garden next, Ellie Mae?"

An alien kitten, maybe? Jax thought mischievously.

"Do I know Howard?" asked her mum.

"He's in my class. He came to the launch with his mum and dad. His dad said your café was the most exciting thing that had ever happened in Goose Green."

Mum nodded. "I remember Howard's dad! He's got a really loud voice. I don't think Howard said a word."

"Howard is a very quiet person," Jax said. Quiet, and somehow just a tiny bit weird, but Jax always felt that it was an *interesting* kind of weird.

"I won't be long!" she told her mum.

But as Jax turned to go, her mum said firmly, "You're not going anywhere with that grass stain on your behind, Ellie Mae. Go and make yourself decent this minute."

"Like Howard's going to see grass stains through all his hair! And for the billionth time, I prefer to be called 'Jax'!" Jax called cheekily as she raced off to change.

Upstairs, she put on clean cut-offs and quickly tidied her hair. Jax was just passing her window when she caught a surprise glimpse of purple. Howard was outside in his garden. For some reason he was dressed in a swirly purple cloak.

Yup, a tiny bit weird, she decided.

Howard seemed anxious as he hunted around in the bushes. *He's realized his rabbit is missing*, Jax thought. *I'd better hurry.* Jax knew how she worried about Beans – and he was a magic moon cat who could look after himself! She flew downstairs and out of the café, and went racing around the corner to Howard's house.

She dashed up the steps to the front door and was just about to bang on the knocker when she heard music floating out through an open window. It sounded dreamy and really sad, Jax thought. Suddenly a woman's voice said, "No, Tabitha, it should go like this." She sang a little bit of the tune Jax had just heard, then the music started up again. Up to that moment Jax had assumed she was listening to a CD!

She lifted the big brass knocker and banged on the door. Nothing happened, so she banged louder. Someone definitely heard that time, because the music broke off with a loud screech that set Jax's teeth on edge.

Angry footsteps came hurrying. An older girl opened the door, gripping her violin as if she wanted to bash Jax with it. "What is it?" she snapped.

Jax heard the unseen woman saying, "Could you try that bit again, Tabby, while we're waiting for Saskia?" That must be Howard's mum, Jax thought. The music started up again, but just the piano and cello were playing this time, without the violin.

"I'm sorry if I'm interrupting," Jax said politely, "but Howard's rabbit is in our garden."

"You'd better come in," said Saskia, still scowling. She stomped off down some stairs, leaving Jax wondering if she should follow. "Well, come on!" Saskia snapped, without bothering to turn round.

Jax followed her down to a big family kitchen, where two identical curly-haired little girls were standing on stools, carefully spreading fairy cakes with bright pink icing. "Good girl, Freya!" their dad was saying in his booming voice. "Wow, Flossie! You managed that all by yourself!" He suddenly spotted Jax. "Hello, young lady, where have you sprung from?"

"I'm Jax," she explained shyly. "My mum runs the Dream Café."

"Howie's rabbit's escaped." Saskia rolled her eyes at her dad.

"Howard and that ridiculous rabbit," Howard's dad muttered half to himself.

Saskia marched over to a pair of French doors and threw them open. "Howie!" she screeched. She tossed her head like an irritable pony. "My brother's hopeless," she complained. "He never comes when he's called. Look, will *you* tell him, whatever-your-name-is? Tabby and I have to practise our piece for the talent show."

She ran back upstairs without waiting for a reply. Jax looked at Howard's dad, but he was helping the twins put sprinkles on their cakes, so she just slipped out into the garden.

She could see Howard at the bottom of the garden, peering around in some bushes. "Howard!" she called. "It's me, Jax!"

In her hurry to tell him the good news she almost tripped over an enormous red box that someone had left in the middle of the grass. On the box, in glittery writing, it said: *MISTER MAGICK. Everything the young magician needs to get started. Amaze your friends with these simple but effective tricks.*

The lid to the box was half open so Jax peered in, curious to see the contents. There was an old-fashioned top hat, a stick with a sparkly tip that she assumed was a wand, a pack of cards,

 some gaudy silk scarves, two
small bunches of artificial
flowers, and a book
with a purple cover
that was sprinkled with
shiny little stars.

"Howard!" she called again. "I've found
your rabbit!"

This time he heard and came bounding
over. When he saw that Jax was by herself he
looked dismayed. "Hubble's okay, isn't he?"

"He's fine," she reassured him. "I would
have brought him but I got kicked by a friend's
rabbit once and I was scared I'd drop him."

"Rabbits can really kick, can't they?"
Howard agreed. "Is it okay if I come and get
him?" Without waiting for an answer, he loped
over to a tall gate in the wall, and Jax saw that
his cloak was sprinkled with stars too, just like

the Mister Magick book.

"Shouldn't you tell your parents?" she asked as he slid back the bolt to the gate.

He shrugged. "They're probably busy. Anyway, I'll be back before anyone notices."

Jax had never heard Howard say so many words at any one time! Maybe it was being at school that made him so shy, she thought. She wondered if he'd remembered that he was wearing a cloak. To remind him, she said tactfully, "Did you get that cloak with your magic set?"

But he just nodded. "My Uncle Gus got me the set for my birthday."

"Wow, what a cool present!" Jax said, though she was secretly doubtful. Having shared her home with a magical moon cat, she didn't think magic was something you could just buy in a box.

Howard had longer legs than Jax so she had to hurry to keep up. "Is your rabbit really called Hubble?" she asked breathlessly.

He nodded. "He's named after a famous telescope."

"The Hubble Space Telescope, I know," Jax said at once. "I've seen some pictures it took of outer space."

Howard looked startled. "I didn't know you were interested in space."

Jax gave him a shy smile. "I love everything to do with space. I've got a telescope in my bedroom, but you can't see stars that well from Goose Green."

"Too many street lamps," Howard agreed. "You need to be out in the desert, or in the middle of the ocean, to see stars clearly."

I'm actually having a conversation with Howard, Jax thought suddenly and she felt so shocked that for a few seconds she was totally tongue-tied. It seemed that Howard felt the same, because he was suddenly tongue-tied at the exact same minute!

Then he said shyly, "Have you really got your own telescope?" and at the same moment Jax said, "So why did you call him Hubble?"

They both giggled, embarrassed, then Howard said, "No, you first."

"I just wondered why you called your rabbit after a space telescope," Jax said.

"Because he looks exactly like a Hubble," Howard explained.

"Actually he totally does!" Jax agreed, laughing. She was

surprised to notice they had already reached the café. She and Howard had been so busy talking, it felt like they'd got there in just a blink.

Howard followed Jax through the café and out into the tiny back garden. Jax was relieved to see Hubble still hopping about, nibbling at her mum's herbs. When Howard picked him up, he still had a sprig of Mum's parsley in his mouth. "Sorry about that," Howard said awkwardly. "Hubble's seriously into parsley."

Beans came trotting up to say hello. He rubbed himself against Howard's legs, purring and doing friendly twirls. "This is my kitten, Beans," Jax said.

"I've seen him in the café," Howard said. "He has a big purr, doesn't he?"

Jax gave a nervous giggle. "Do you think?"

She suddenly noticed that Hubble seemed to be looking down at Beans from Howard's arms and Beans was most *definitely* looking up at Hubble. For a moment, it seemed like the pet rabbit and the little moon cat were actually talking. Before Jax could wonder about this, Howard said abruptly, "I'd better go. I still need to practise loads."

Jax hadn't realized Howard was a musician like his sisters. "What instrument do you play?" she asked.

"I don't play any instruments." Howard had turned bright red. "I meant I need to practise my magic. It's only three weeks till the talent show."

"You're actually entering the talent show?" Jax couldn't hide her surprise.

"What's wrong with that?" Howard snapped.

Because you're so incredibly shy, Jax thought. But she couldn't say that to Howard so she said awkwardly, "Oh, um, no reason."

"Well, that's what I'll be doing," Howard told her stiffly. "I'm going to be Mister Magick so, like I said, I really need to practise. Thanks for finding Hubble," he added in the same unfriendly voice and, with a swirl of his cloak, he was gone.

Later that afternoon, Mum called to Jax to come downstairs. "The vet just rang to say she's on her way," she said smiling. "I thought while she was here we'd get her to look at Beans."

Jax felt a flash of cold panic. Suppose the vet noticed he wasn't a normal cat? "But B-Beans isn't ill!" she stuttered.

"It still won't hurt to get him checked out," Mum said cheerfully.

Jax could feel her heart jumping in her chest. "I'm not sure if we shut the shed door," she gabbled. "We don't want the vet to come all this way to find Rumble's wandered off."

She flew out to the shed, where Beans was having a friendly nap with Rumble. "Beans, the vet's coming!" Jax's breath was coming in panicky gasps. "You mustn't let her see you!"

The little moon cat opened his eyes and blinked at her in surprise. *Why not?*

"*Think* about it! You could have, like, an extra heart or something and she'll suss you're from another world."

I don't have an extra heart, he said coolly. *I have exactly the right number of hearts for a moon cat.*

"That's SO not helpful, Beans, seeing as I have no idea how many hearts that is!" Jax was whispering for Rumble's sake, but she wanted to scream and shout, she was so stressed.

I have just one heart, the same as you, Beans reassured her.

"But you do all those different purrs and you have moon-cat stripes and sparkles in your fur. We can't take the *risk*!" Jax was wringing her hands.

Moonbeans came to rub his head lovingly against her bare ankles. *I'll make myself invisible if you're worried*, he promised.

Jax almost cried with relief. "Thank you, Beans!" It was her darkest fear that someone would recognize her little alien cat for what he truly was and then she would lose him for ever.

The café was quiet by the time the vet turned up, the teatime rush not having started.

When Rumble woke to see everyone crowding into the shed, he backed even further into his cardboard fortress, spitting and hissing, and refusing to be coaxed out.

Since she couldn't examine him, the vet couldn't say for sure what was wrong with Rumble, but she thought it was a bad case of cat flu. She told Jax and her mum that they were doing all the right things, making sure he had clean water, and tempting him with tiny treats, and she said she'd leave some pills that might help. The vet showed them how to mash one of the pills into Rumble's sardines, but when she carefully pushed the dish into his cardboard-box lair, he stonily ignored it.

"He will get better, won't he?" Jax asked anxiously.

"Well, Rumble's obviously a real survivor," the vet said, smiling. "So we shouldn't write him off just yet."

Somewhere in the shadows, Jax heard a familiar purr start up and she couldn't help smiling to herself. Moonbeans was doing his bit to help Rumble recover!

Maybe the vet noticed without realizing because she suddenly said, "Didn't you have another cat you wanted me to take a look at?"

"Yes, I don't know where he's got to," Mum said in surprise. "He usually follows my daughter around everywhere."

The vet picked up her bag. "Then I'll have to see him some other time, I'm afraid. I've got some other house calls to make."

Desperate to get the vet away from the shed, which was becoming alarmingly pink and fizzy, Jax hastily led the way outside.

After the gloom of the shed, the afternoon sunshine made Jax blink. As her eyes adjusted to the light, she was startled to see crowds of brightly coloured butterflies fluttering in and out of the flowers.

The vet looked amazed. "Who knew there were so many butterflies in Goose Green!"

"Mum plants butterfly-friendly plants to attract them, that's why," Jax said quickly; though she secretly suspected that the butterflies were more attracted to the fizzy

moon vibes leaking from their garden shed. Jax grinned to herself. This time Beans had seriously overdone the Purr of Power.

Before she went to bed that night, Jax called in to check on Rumble. To her relief, he didn't growl or spit, just glared balefully from his cardboard fortress. Jax frowned down at the saucer of sardines and decided there was a tiny cat-sized mouthful missing. "Listen, Mr Fighter Cat," she told him. "I know you're used to being the boss cat but you've been *really* poorly so you have to let me and Beans look after you till you're better."

Rumble blinked his gummy eyes at her and Jax had the strangest feeling he was listening. "Oh, and I forgot to say my mum says you can stay for as long as you want," she added. "So don't worry, okay? See you tomorrow." Jax

carefully closed the door of the shed.

In the garden it was getting dark and all the daisies had closed their petals. Jax crouched down to pick one just as Beans trotted out of the dusk. *I heard you talking to Rumble*, he told her.

Jax felt embarrassed that she'd been

overheard. "I know he isn't our mission, but I can still be nice," she told him.

It was a warm evening and suddenly Jax didn't feel like going back indoors. She perched on the bench that her mum had painted to match the shed and patted the seat. "Let's talk!"

Beans sprang up beside her. *What about?*

Jax tickled his nose with her daisy. "You know what about, you cheeky moon cat – our real mission! It's Hubble, isn't it? He escaped on purpose. He asked you to help him."

You're sure you're not turning into a moon cat? Beans teased. *You're almost right. Hubble wants us to help Howard.*

Jax gasped. "Is Howard in trouble then?"

He will be if he enters that talent show. Hubble wants us to stop him.

Jax was shocked. "That's not a mission, that's just mean!"

It isn't mean, Beans said sharply. *Hubble wants Howard to be happy and he doesn't think doing magic tricks in front of the school will make Howard happy.*

Jax remembered thinking that Beans and Hubble were having a conversation. So she hadn't imagined it. They were actually talking about Howard! "So did he tell you about Howard and his Mister Magick kit?" Jax wished she could have eavesdropped on *that* conversation!

Yes. Howard's using Hubble in his act, so he's seen Howard do all the tricks in his Mister Magick book and he says he's a terrible magician.

"That's *so* not fair! Hubble's just got to give him time," Jax objected. "Howard says himself that he needs more practice. Plus he's still got three weeks to improve."

Hubble doesn't think that's long enough. He

says his tricks go wrong every time.

"I'm sorry, but isn't it Howard's business if he wants to enter the talent show!" Jax said fiercely. "I think it's incredibly brave of him to go up onstage, especially since he's so shy, and it would be *really* cruel to stop him."

Is it cruel to stop him from embarrassing himself in front of the school and his entire family?

"Well, no," said Jax, "but—"

Hubble says Howard has absolutely no confidence as it is. If he fails in public, Hubble thinks it will totally crush him.

Jax sat thoughtfully stroking Beans, as the velvety twilight stole over the garden. "I get why Hubble's worried," she said at last. "I mean, Howard's his human. Naturally he doesn't want him to mess up in front of everybody. But stopping Howard doing his act just seems wrong."

Beans blinked his amber eyes at her. *What do you think we should do?*

"I think we should help him be a success," Jax said firmly.

How can we do that if he's no good? Beans asked.

Jax was pulling the petals off her daisy without realizing. She was remembering how, when she went to Howard's house, his mum had been upstairs helping his big sisters with their music, while his dad was downstairs decorating cakes with Howard's little sisters. Howard had been all by himself, hunting around the garden for his lost rabbit.

"I think I know why Howard is so desperate to be Mister Magick," she told Beans suddenly. "He's not a musical genius like Tabitha or Saskia, and he's way too old to be cute like Flossie and Freya, so it's like he doesn't really count."

Beans gave her bare elbow a friendly lick. *Do you remember I told you about that time I got stuck being invisible and the Aunts had to turn me back? I think Howard must feel like he's invisible.*

"But there's nobody to turn him back," Jax said softly and she felt a tiny ache in her heart for lonely Howard.

Beans was watching her with interest. *You like Howard, don't you?*

Jax felt herself blushing in the dark. "I don't exactly *like* him. I just think he deserves to have somebody on his side."

He has Hubble, Beans pointed out. *Hubble came to ask for our help, remember?*

"I know that, Beans, but I meant someone human."

Hubble might just be a big fat rabbit to you,

Beans almost snapped, *but it took a lot of courage for him to come here. He got chased by a dog and he almost ran into a mower. He could have been hurt.*

Beans was cross with her for not taking Hubble seriously, Jax realized. "I didn't know about the dog," she said humbly. "That was really brave."

"There you are!" Mum had come out to look for Jax. "What are you and Beans doing sitting out here in the dark?"

"Oh, we were just planning our next mission!" Jax giggled to let her mum know that this was a joke. "I'm a girl superhero, didn't you know?"

"Oh, *really!*" Mum was laughing too, not

believing a word of it. "So Beans must be your sidekick then?"

Jax slid a mischievous glance at Beans. "It's Saturday so I'm the sidekick today. Beans only gets to be the superhero on Saturdays, don't you, Beans?"

Very funny. Ha ha ha, he told her.

That night Jax dreamed about Howard doing his magic tricks in front of a booing crowd. She woke with a gasp and immediately felt around for Beans, but he wasn't there. He must have gone out on the prowl.

Not wanting to go back to sleep in case she had another bad dream, Jax got up and padded restlessly over to her window. She was surprised to see a light on upstairs in Howard's house across the gardens.

That's Howard's room, she thought, and felt a

pang of worry. Jax pictured him anxiously practising his magic tricks while the rest of his family were sleeping. "Oh, Howard," she said softly. *You don't actually know he's practising magic*, she comforted herself. *He might just be reading his space books.*

Jax knew it was wrong to spy on people, but she was on an important mission and she suddenly needed to see for herself. Swivelling her dad's telescope so it was pointing at Howard's window, she put her eye to the lens.

She caught her breath as Howard came clearly into view. Wearing his striped pyjamas, he was carefully fanning out a deck of playing cards. Jax had seen a stage magician do the same thing just before he asked a member of the audience to pick a card. But the stage magician didn't drop all his cards and he didn't have to scrabble around for ages picking them

 up either. Jax felt her stomach clench as Howard crawled around collecting  up the cards and got ready to start his trick all over again. She had a dreadful feeling that Howard had been bravely picking up cards and dropping them for *hours*.

 Suddenly he threw down the cards and buried his face in his hands.

Jax quickly took her eye away from the telescope. But for a long while she stood shivering in her pyjamas, watching Howard's brightly lit window, and wondering how in the world she and Beans could help him.

Thank you for ruining my life!

6

It was Monday morning and Jax was getting ready for school. She'd been awake half the night trying to think of a way to turn shy, clumsy Howard into a successful and confident stage magician.

"There is *one* way we could help Howard." She slid a sly look at Beans as she buttoned up her skirt.

No, he said firmly.

Jax rolled her eyes. "Could you just once pretend you can't read my mind and let me tell you my idea."

No, because I can *read your mind*, said Beans. *You know I can't use moon magic to cheat.*

"It wouldn't be *actual* cheating! You'd just turn yourself invisible and sit in the audience with me, do the Purr of Power and make Howard's act look incredibly cool. Who's it going to hurt?"

It will hurt Howard, said Beans.

"I don't see why!" she said indignantly. "It's not like Howard is doing *real* magic. It's only conjuring tricks! You'd just be helping him look good!"

Howard doesn't need someone to make him "look" good. Beans was disapproving. *He needs to know he IS good.*

"So basically it's an impossible mission and we might as well give up! Thanks for nothing, Beans!" Jax stormed over to the window and stood glaring out over the gardens.

Okay, so it wasn't such a great plan, but it was the only one she had. Howard needed their help and Jax couldn't bear the thought that they might let him down. A moment later she felt the little moon cat brush against her ankles. *Remember how we helped Ruby-Rose? Remember what you did?*

Jax blew out her breath. "Yeah, yeah, I had to get to know her before she'd trust me. So now you're saying I've got to get to know Howard?"

Beans just went on purring, waiting for Jax to figure it out for herself.

"It's all right for moon cats," she grumbled. "Humans have to *talk* to each other."

You talked to Howard, Beans reminded her.

Jax sat down to pull on her socks. "That was before."

Beans looked puzzled. *Before what?*

"Before I knew what a huge deal this was for him. What if I say something dumb? I could make him feel even *more* of a failure!" Jax felt close to tears.

Moonbeans closed his eyes as he purred. For a moment he looked like he was smiling.

"You're going to tell me to just listen to my heart, aren't you?" Jax sighed.

He bumped his nose against hers. *It works for moon cats.*

Jax was finally ready for school. She picked up her bag. "Wish me luck!"

"Earth to Jax!" Lilia teased at break time. "I've been talking for ages and you haven't heard a word I've said!"

"Sorry," said Jax. "I've got something on my mind."

"Is it about the talent show?" Lilia asked hopefully.

"Yes and no," Jax said. "I mean it *is* about the talent show but not how you mean."

Lilia rolled her eyes. "You've been eating too much space dust," she joked. "You're making absolutely NO sense!"

Jax took a breath. "Can you keep a secret?"

"Oh, *yes*!" Lilia said, beaming. "I can SO totally keep a secret. I've known for ages about Ruby-Rose and Conrad fancying each other and I never told anyone!" She clapped her hand to her mouth. "Oops!"

Everybody in the whole school knew Ruby-Rose and Conrad fancied each other, but Jax didn't say this to Lilia.

"So what's the secret?" Lilia asked eagerly.

Jax hesitated. She wasn't sure if Howard would want her to tell anybody, but Lilia sometimes had really helpful ideas. "Howard's entering the talent show," Jax said in a rush. "He's doing a magic act." The moment the words were out of her mouth she wanted to take them back.

Lilia stared at her. "But Howard hardly even *talks!*"

"I know," Jax said. "That's why—"

"Well, I think he's *really* brave!" Lilia interrupted.

"I *know* that," said Jax impatiently. "The point is I saw Howard practising in the garden," she fibbed, "and I don't think magic tricks are, you know, his best thing."

But Lilia didn't seem to be listening. "You know, it's so weird but I can totally picture Howard being a magician!" she babbled.

"Do you think he needs an assistant? I would LOVE to be a magician's assistant." She flashed a naughty grin. "Do you dare me to ask him?"

"No! I just *told* you it's a secret!"

Lilia suddenly had a stubborn look in her eye. "So? You're the one who told me I should find someone else who wanted to enter the show. This could be my one chance to be in it. I'm going to call him over now."

"Lilia, you *mustn't*!" Jax was sure this was a very bad idea.

"Why mustn't I?" Lilia started waving wildly. "Hey, Howard, come here!"

Howard looked around the playground to see who Lilia was talking to, even though he was the only boy in the entire school called Howard. Then he reluctantly made his way over.

Unfortunately Lilia's courage ran out the minute Howard was standing in front of her.

She went bright pink and shot a pleading look at Jax. "Can you ask him for me?" she whispered.

Jax couldn't see any way out of this unless she dug an extremely big hole down to Australia, so she just blurted out, "Lilia wants to know if she can be your assistant in your magic act."

Howard looked appalled. "What did you tell Lilia for? Nobody in my family even knows. I was going to surprise them on the night."

"But have you got an assistant, though?" Lilia persisted.

"I don't need an assistant!" Howard was using the stiff voice he used when he was stressed. "I've got Hubble."

"Who's Hubble?" Lilia whispered to Jax.

"His rabbit," Jax whispered back.

"So he hasn't got an actual assistant then?" Lilia checked with Jax.

"No," said Howard. "But—"

"So if he hasn't got an assistant, who is he going to saw in half?" Lilia hissed to Jax as if Howard wasn't there.

"I'm not sawing anyone in half, Lilia!" Howard was seriously stressed now. "For one thing, I haven't got a saw, plus I wouldn't dream of attempting those advanced kinds of tricks."

"My brother's got a saw you can borrow," said a cheerful voice. Conrad had sneaked up when they weren't looking.

Jax saw Howard close his eyes. Now THREE people knew his secret. She hastily tried to smooth things over. "Conrad, you won't tell anybody, will you?"

Conrad solemnly drew his finger across his throat. "Silent as the grave, that's me!"

"But can I be your assistant though, if I promise not to tell anyone?" Lilia said, sounding like a stuck CD.

"I'll be your MC if you like," Conrad suggested. "You know, that guy who gets the audience warmed up before the acts come on."

Howard was looking desperate. "I don't think—"

"Go on," Conrad pleaded. "I'd introduce you like this." He cupped his hands around his mouth and bellowed, "Please give a warm welcome to the SPECTACULAR, the ONE and ONLY – what are you calling yourself?"

"Mister Magick," Howard said. "But it's supposed to be a—"

"Please give a warm welcome to the one and only, SPECTACULAR, SPELLBINDING MISTER MAGICK!" Everybody turned to look as Conrad's voice carried right across the playground. Even Howard's big sisters spun around in surprise.

"…secret," Howard mumbled. "Only now everybody in the school knows, including my sisters, so thank you, Conrad. Thank you very much for ruining my life!"

Jax felt her heart sinking into her shoes as Howard stormed off around the corner and out of sight. How could something go so wrong, so fast? Why had she even told Lilia about Howard's magic show? Howard would never be her friend now and she didn't blame him. If she was Howard, she wouldn't want to be friends with her either. And now she had to go home and tell Beans that she'd already blown their new mission.

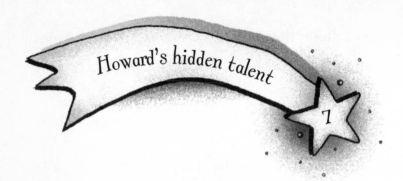

"I've ruined *everything*, Beans! After today, Howard is never going to trust me ever again and I don't blame him. Everybody in the school knows he's doing a magic act, so even if he *wanted* to change his mind, he's *got* to go through with it now! He's under more pressure than he was *before*! Which means it'll be even *harder* for him to get his tricks right."

Jax was wringing her hands she was so upset. Beans had been out prowling all evening and had only come in through the cat flap as Jax was putting on her PJs, getting ready for

bed. She had waited so long to confess that it all came pouring out the minute poor little Beans came trotting into her room!

Talking was supposed to make you feel better, but as Jax went on describing what had happened, she just felt more and more ashamed of herself.

"Why did I have to tell Lilia?" she wailed. "I'm just a big old blabbermouth, Beans. Conrad's worse though!" she added with a shudder. The memory made her cover her face. "I couldn't believe it when he shouted it out in front of the whole school! I wanted to crawl into a hole and die!"

Beans rubbed his furry face against hers. *It'll be all right.*

"You keep saying that! But you never ever say *how*!" Jax was almost crying now.

At that exact moment she looked out of her window and saw Howard in his Mister Magick cloak making his way slowly back up the garden towards his house. The sun had almost set and the stars on his cloak glimmered in the dusk. Jax felt a strange little shiver go through her, because, from a distance and just for a moment, Howard actually did look a tiny bit magic.

Everybody is a bit magic once you know them, Beans said, reading her mind. *We just need to help Howard find his own special type of magic.*

Jax turned, surprised. "Do you mean like a hidden talent?"

Humans say talent. Moon cats call it magic,
Beans said.

"It doesn't really matter what we call it,
since Howard is refusing to talk to me," Jax
reminded him.

*Then you'd better find a way to make him talk
to you,* Beans said cheerfully. *Maybe you could
take him some of those cosmic cupcakes?* Nadia's
newest creations were now on sale at the
Dream Café.

"I think it's going to take more than
cupcakes." Jax gave him a sheepish grin. "I
think it might take something like a moon cat
with a very special purr," she hinted. "Or would
that count as cheating?"

Beans thought for a moment. *No, that
wouldn't count as cheating.*

"I'll *really* try not to blow it this time," Jax
promised.

Next morning, Howard refused to even look at Jax. In the playground at lunchtime, he just stalked right by her and her friends.

"Howard will never let me be in his magic act now," Lilia moaned.

Ruby-Rose's eyes went wide. "Is Howard seriously planning to do a magic act?"

"Ssh," Jax told her fiercely. "He doesn't like people talking about it."

"So why was Conrad yelling about it to the whole school?" asked Ruby-Rose.

"Because I'm a numpty?" Conrad suggested. He pulled a face at Ruby-Rose. "Plus I was auditioning to be his MC."

"I was going to be his assistant," said Lilia wistfully.

"Could *I* be one?" asked Ruby-Rose at once.

"Have you got a sparkly outfit?" asked Lilia.

"I've got loads from all those dance shows I used to do. I'll lend you one if you like. Plus, if Conrad's going to be Howard's MC, he needs a flash waistcoat."

"How flash are we talking?" Conrad said with interest.

Ruby-Rose grinned at him. "Just flash enough to make you super-cool."

It was like being in the middle of a mad tennis match, Jax thought, as her friends bounced excited comments back and forth. Without him knowing, Mister Magick had acquired a Master of Ceremonies and *two* glamorous girl assistants. She had a moment's panic as her and Beans's mission went galloping out of control.

Then she suddenly had the most sweetly

tingly feeling, as if the Aunts were smiling down at her from their little planet with five moons. Even Jax was smiling – she had no idea why! She still didn't have a plan; yet she felt as if everything was working out just the way it should.

This feeling stayed with her till home time as she headed back to the café. And she still felt tingly and happy as she set off for Howard's, with her invisible moon cat and a Tupperware box filled with cosmic cupcakes.

"I love going on missions, don't you?" Jax said happily.

It's one of my favourite things in the universe, Beans agreed.

The same dreamy music Jax had heard

before was pouring out of the open window as she and Beans hurried up the steps to Howard's front door. Jax plucked up her courage and banged the door extra hard with the big brass knocker. This time Howard's other big sister, Tabitha, answered the door.

Jax politely explained that she'd come to see Howard.

"You mean, my *brother* Howard? Are you sure?" Tabitha sounded every bit as scornful as Saskia.

"I'm quite sure, thank you," Jax said, wishing she could give Tabitha's hair a super-hard yank.

Without moving, Tabitha yelled, "Howard! Your girlfriend's coming up to see you!"

Jax carefully counted to ten. "I'm a girl and I'm Howard's friend," she told Tabitha firmly. "That doesn't mean I'm his girlfriend. You'll embarrass him, saying things like that."

"Howie!" Tabitha yelled immediately. "She says she's a friend and she's a girl but she's absolutely *not* your girlfriend."

Jax felt Beans brush invisibly against her ankles. She knew they were thinking the same thing; no wonder Howard didn't have any confidence, with those girls for sisters!

Halfway up the stairs, Jax heard the thump of rock music. She followed the sound of drums and guitars until her ears were seriously hurting, and by then she'd found Howard's room. She knocked and went right in.

Howard spun around in shock and Jax saw that he had a magician's silk scarf poking out of his sleeve. "Oh, it's you," he said grumpily. He picked up the remote for his stereo.

"Don't switch it off, I like it," Jax fibbed, raising her voice over the racket. With loud music playing, Beans could do his Purr of

Power without Howard hearing. She looked around Howard's room, noticing that he had some of the same space posters she had on her wall. "Where's Hubble?" she asked.

"He's here." Howard moved aside and Jax saw his rabbit snoozing on a piece of folded blanket on the floor.

Jax hadn't known that rabbits could sleep through loud rock music, or that they could fall asleep with all their paws sticking up in the air. "He looks cute," she giggled.

"I don't want to be rude." Howard was using his stiff voice again. "But I haven't really got time to chat. I need to practise my act."

"That's partly why I came – to talk about your act," Jax said quickly. "I was hoping you'd changed your mind about having Lilia and Conrad in your act. Actually, Ruby-Rose wants to be in it too," she added with a grin.

Howard looked appalled. "I already told you, I don't want any girl assistants and I *definitely* don't want Conrad to be my MC."

"Okay," said Jax meekly. "Well, I mainly stopped by to bring you some of Lilia's mum's cosmic cupcakes. I wanted to make it up to you for blabbing your secret to everybody." She set a plastic box on the table next to Howard's Mister Magick stuff and opened the lid.

Howard stared down at the cupcakes. He looked puzzled. "Sorry," he yelled over the music, "but I don't see how a cupcake can be *cosmic*."

"It's because they've got space dust in," Jax yelled back. "It's a harmless chemical that explodes in your head!"

"Seriously?" For the first time, Howard looked interested.

He picked up a cake and took a very small bite. Jax giggled at his expressions as the space dust instantly exploded in his mouth. "How weird is *that*?" he said to himself and immediately took another bite. Unlike Jax, Howard was a slow, careful eater. He made his cupcake last so long that Jax was ready to scream.

"Your mum seriously gave you all those for me?" Howard said, still munching.

"Unless you fancy sharing them," Jax hinted.

"Sure, help yourself," he said awkwardly.

"You've got loads of space books," Jax said approvingly as she munched. "Can I see if we've got the same ones?"

"If you want," Howard said. "How come you're so into space, anyway?"

Jax took down a book at random. "My dad was a scientist. He was telling me about the universe when I was still in my high chair."

"So where's your dad? I don't think I've ever seen him."

"Oh, he died when I was six. It's just me and Mum now."

Howard flushed. "Sorry, I didn't know."

"That's okay." Jax turned over a page. "*Supernova,*" she read aloud. "*Nebulae. Solar winds.* Those will always be Dad words to me!" She gave Howard a shy smile. "I always think they're kind of like poetry."

"You're almost as weird as me," Howard told her, with his mouth full of exploding cupcake. "My sisters are always saying I'm weird. Do you think I'm weird?" he asked abruptly.

Jax looked at Howard in his Mister Magick cloak with space dust crackling in his mouth, and had to bite her lip so she wouldn't laugh. "Do you want a truthful answer?"

Howard burst out laughing, and Jax realized it was the first time she'd seen him laugh. "What is it about me that strikes you as weird, Ellie Mae?" he said, putting on a funny voice. He clutched at his throat. "Help, I've been taken over by aliens. Give me my voice back, you naughty aliens!"

"Why do people always think aliens want to take them over?" Jax said irritably. Then she saw Howard's hurt expression and wished she could take it back. "I liked your funny voice though," she told him quickly. "What do you think Hubble would sound like if he could talk?"

Howard immediately put on a whiffly rabbit voice. "What do you mean, *if* I can talk! I am the original talking genius rabbit, man!"

Jax hooted with laughter. "You're brilliant at voices!"

Howard shook his head. "I'm not brilliant at anything."

"My mum says everyone's brilliant at something," Jax said. "You just have to find the right something."

Howard let out a sigh. "I'm not sure there *is* a 'right something'. I've tried everything. Mister Magick is my last chance."

"Your last chance to do what?" Jax asked, puzzled.

Suddenly Howard couldn't meet her eyes. "To make my family proud of me."

Jax sat down beside Hubble, stroking his

long ears. Howard's room was getting seriously pink and shimmery and the fizzy sensation in her tummy told her that Beans was doing his Purr of Power. "What other ways have you tried?" she asked sympathetically.

Howard started counting on his fingers. "First there was the school choir. But it turns out I've got a voice like a foghorn!"

"Oh, I'm sure you haven't—" Jax started.

"No, I totally have!" Howard threw back his head and let out such a terrible groaning sound that Jax had to cover her ears. "The teacher was ever so nice about it," Howard said with a sigh. "She just asked if I could sing *really* quietly. I think she was worried some passing oil tanker would get wrecked on our playground!"

Jax stared at him, open-mouthed. She had never realized before, but Howard was *funny*! "So what did you try after the choir?" she asked.

He started ticking them off on his fingers. "I played the drums in the school orchestra. I tried out for the athletics team. I—" Jax realized that Howard wasn't really thinking about what he was saying. He had started looking around with a puzzled expression. "Can you hear a cat purring?"

Oh-oh, Jax thought. The music had stopped without her noticing. "It's probably Beans," she said in a casual voice. "That little kitty follows me everywhere. Come out, kitty!" she cooed. "Where are you hiding?"

Moonbeans's furry face peeped out from under Howard's bed. A big blob of dust hung off one of his whiskers. Jax could tell he was *really* embarrassed at being discovered. She quickly gathered him into her arms. His fur was standing up like dandelion fluff. That always happened when Beans materialized too quickly. *It was my fault*, she told him in her head. *I didn't notice the music had stopped.* Out loud she said, "I'd better take this naughty kitty back home. Um, good luck with the magic tricks."

"Oh, thanks," said Howard awkwardly. "Thanks for the cupcakes," he called after her.

It was my fault, Beans said forlornly on the way home. *I got carried away doing my Purr of Power. It all seemed to be going so well.*

"It's okay," Jax told him. Everybody in the universe made mistakes, she thought. Even magic moon cats. "Let's go and see how Rumble's doing," she suggested.

115

You go, said Beans dejectedly. *I need to be alone for a while.*

Rumble was fast asleep. Jax was impressed to see that both his saucers, which she'd carefully refilled, morning and night, were polished clean. For the first time, he'd drunk every drop of water and gobbled every single scrap of sardine, along with the vet's medicine.

And something else was different, she thought, frowning. Suddenly she realized what it was. He wasn't wheezing!

"Oh, Rumble, that's so brilliant! You're getting better!" she exclaimed softly.

At the sound of her voice, Rumble opened his eyes, and for just an instant she saw it – that magic spark that Beans said everybody had inside. And at the exact same instant, Rumble saw the magic spark inside *her*! Jax could feel it. The human girl and the homeless cat silently gazed at each other. Then Rumble closed his eyes and Jax tiptoed away.

After supper Jax settled down in her room to do her homework. Tapping her pencil against her teeth, she tried to concentrate on the maths problems Mrs. Chaudhary had set them. Then a car horn suddenly sounded down in the street and she unexpectedly found herself picturing an oil tanker running aground in the playground, lured by Howard's terrible foghorn voice, and she went off into fits of laughter.

Beans looked up. *What's funny?*

"Howard," Jax said, still giggling. "He is the funniest boy I have ever met!" Then she gasped. "Beans, I've got it!"

She had figured out Howard's hidden talent!

Seriously mysterious

8

That night, Jax and Beans stayed awake, talking. City noises floated in through the open window, mixed with smells of traffic fumes and takeaways. Jax knew what she had to do. She had to persuade Howard to swap his terrible magic act for something he did really well – making people laugh. She just didn't know *how*.

"I can't just come out and tell him he's a comedy genius," Jax said. "He'll think it's a wind-up."

Then you'll have to show him, said Beans.

"I know," said Jax. "But that means finding an audience."

Jax could see Beans's amber-gold eyes glowing in the dark. *It doesn't have to be a big audience*, he pointed out.

"I suppose I could ask Conrad and Lilia and Ruby-Rose." It was a big gamble, Jax thought. What if Howard was only funny before because it was just Jax there? What if he totally clammed up in front of the others?

You know what I think, Beans told her. *I think we just have to believe in Howard.*

Jax propped herself up on her elbow. "The Aunts believe in him, don't they?" She pictured them smiling down from the little planet with five moons, saying, *You're almost there, Jax and Beans. Don't give up now!*

We won't, Jax promised silently. She couldn't give up, because somehow, without

119

her noticing, Howard had become her friend.

It turned out that Howard also thought of Jax as *his* friend. She was still in her pyjamas next morning when her mum came in with the phone. "Howard needs to ask you something."

Jax tried to sound super-casual. "Oh, hi, Howard."

She heard him take a deep breath. "I need a favour. Could you help me practise my magic tricks? It's getting really close to the talent show now and I'm…well, you probably noticed," he said ruefully, "I'm getting a bit stressed."

Jax couldn't believe this shy boy was asking for her help. "Sure," she said, swallowing. "I'll come round to yours straight after school."

Jax suddenly knew that she and Beans were thinking the same thing: this was the *perfect* opportunity they needed to fulfil their mission!

Tell him you're bringing the others, Beans prompted.

"*Give me a chance!*" she mouthed. "Um, Howard, there's just one thing. I'll be bringing the others."

"No! I just want it to be you!" Jax heard panic in Howard's voice.

"Howard, trust me," she said firmly. "It'll be heaps better with the others there. Plus Ruby-Rose knows all about performing, so she can give you tips."

There was a long silence.

"Okay," Howard agreed reluctantly. Then he added fiercely, "But they'd better not *laugh*."

"Okay!" Jax's voice came out in a squeak,

she was trying so hard not to giggle. It wasn't
an actual fib, though, because she'd quickly
crossed her fingers.

At morning break, Jax took her friends to a
quiet corner of the playground and explained
that Howard needed their help with his
magic act.

"Cool!" Lilia beamed. "Does that mean
Ruby-Rose and I get to be his assistants?"

"And can I be his MC?" asked Conrad.

"Maybe," Jax said cautiously. "I can't really
explain, but if we're all there to help, I think
Howard's act might sort of *change*."

Conrad grinned at her. "You should be a
secret agent, Jackson!"

"Why?" she said, startled.

"Cos you are being *seriously* mysterious!"
he said, laughing.

For the rest of that day Jax found it impossible to concentrate. She was about to take a huge risk, and she knew that risks didn't always pay off. She really wished Moonbeans could come with them, but she didn't dare let him be discovered twice. The problem was that without Beans to do his Purr of Power, things could get *really* awkward.

Jax and her friends arrived at Howard's house dead on time. Howard's dad opened the door and she saw him blink with surprise.

"We've come to help Howard with his act for the talent show," she explained. "He said it would be all right for us to come round."

"I think he did mention something," he boomed in his jolly Father Christmassy voice. "You'd better go on up." Jax had the feeling

Howard's parents weren't used to Howard having friends.

They found him running his fingers through his hair as he studied his Mister Magick book of tricks. "Oh, hi," he said in a worried voice. "Um, thanks for coming."

Everybody hung around, waiting for someone to say something. Suddenly Conrad yelped. "Flaming Nora, it's a real rabbit! I thought it was stuffed, then I saw it twitch its little nose!"

"Of course he's real," Howard said stiffly. "Why would anyone have a stuffed rabbit? Even I'm not *that* weird."

But Conrad wasn't listening. He was much too fascinated by Hubble. "How come he stays on his blanket instead of hopping around doing bunny poos everywhere?" he asked.

"I trained him," Howard explained. "He stays where I put him till I say he can move."

"I didn't know you could train rabbits!" Ruby-Rose was impressed.

"Hubble's an extremely intelligent rabbit," Howard said in a gloomy voice. "Really, he should be pulling *me* out of a hat."

Conrad burst out laughing. "That's funny, man."

Jax saw that Ruby-Rose and Lilia were laughing too and she held her breath. Her plan-that-wasn't-exactly-a-plan was starting to work.

"I'd pay good money to see that rabbit pulling you out of a hat!" Conrad spluttered.

And as if the Aunts had whispered in her ear, Jax had a sudden brilliant brainwave.

"Howard, I've got an idea for your act," she said daringly.

He looked puzzled. "I've got my act all sorted though." He shot a worried glance at the table with all his Mister Magick gear. "It just needs work. Isn't that why you're all here?"

"I know that, Howard," said Jax cunningly, "but can I just tell you my idea? Because I think you'll love it."

Howard chewed at his lip for a moment. "Okay. Tell me your idea," he said cautiously.

Jax beamed at him. "I think you and Hubble should do a double act!"

Howard stared at her. "A double act? With a rabbit? Are you bonkers? Even Hubble isn't *that* smart!"

"It wouldn't be an *actual* double act, you numpty! You'd just be pretending!"

Ruby-Rose started to grin. "You know what would be funny? If Howard made out their act was, like, all Hubble's idea!"

Howard perked up. "You mean it'd be like Hubble is bossing Mister Magick about? That's actually quite cool," he admitted.

"Do that weird rabbit voice again," Jax said at once.

"Hey, who are you calling weird, dude? Don't go disrespecting me just because I'm a rabbit," Howard said in his Hubble voice.

Conrad let out a shout of laughter. "Bullied by a rabbit. I LOVE it!"

"That could definitely work," Ruby-Rose said, nodding.

"Would he still need girl assistants though?" asked Lilia.

"And an MC?" asked Conrad hopefully.

"Totally," said Jax. "Howard will still come

on like he's Mister Magick, but then his act goes off in a totally different direction."

"Which direction is that?" Howard asked nervously.

Jax's eyes sparkled. "I'm just getting to that."

When Jax eventually got home, her mum was too tired to cook supper, so they ordered a takeaway from the Red Hot Wok. Jax always had the same thing: chicken and crispy noodles. She breathed in the delicious spicy smells as her mum unpacked the steaming cartons.

"I've had an idea," said Mum. "I thought we might invite Grandpa to come with us to the talent show. What do you think?"

Jax threw her arms around her mum.

"That's a brilliant idea!" They hadn't seen her grandpa for months now.

"He probably won't come." Mum sighed. "Maybe you should ask him, Ellie? You can be really persuasive when you want."

Jax grinned to herself, remembering what she had just persuaded Howard into. She pinched a prawn off her mum's plate. "I'll call him tonight!" she promised.

Every afternoon after school, Conrad, Lilia, Jax and Ruby-Rose met at the Dream Café, to help Howard polish his outrageous new act. There were less than two weeks to go until the talent show now, so there was no time to lose.

It had been Jax's idea to have rehearsals in the back room behind the café. She'd explained that it would keep Howard's act a secret from his family. What she didn't say was that Moonbeans could also purr non-stop in the background without people getting suspicious. Although Howard had discovered his hidden talent, he was still the same shy boy inside, and he needed all the magical vibes he could get.

One afternoon, Jax had just popped into the café to fetch some snacks for her friends, when Howard's parents walked in with their little twin girls. She gave them a friendly wave. "Hi! Did you want to see Howard?"

"No, no, we wouldn't want to disturb the rehearsal!" Howard's dad reassured her in his big cheery voice.

"We were hoping your mum might have some of those exciting cosmic cupcakes," Howard's mum explained. "Howard shared his with Flossie and Freya and they rather thought they'd like some more!"

Howard's dad gave Jax a twinkly smile. "But while we're here, perhaps you could shed some light on this mysterious act Howard's doing for the talent show?"

"Not a chance!" said Jax cheekily. "You'll have to wait till Friday like everyone else." She was giggling to herself as she ran back to the others. If Howard's act went according to plan, his parents were going to have the surprise of their lives!

After their last rehearsal, Jax asked Howard to stay behind. "That was your best ever performance," she told him truthfully. "Do it like that tomorrow and everyone will be blown away."

Howard blushed. "Thanks. I never realized how cool it is to make people laugh. It makes you feel – I don't know – *magic!*"

She took a deep breath. "I've just got one other tiny little suggestion."

Jax put down her scissors and led Howard to a mirror. He stared at himself for a long minute. "I look all right," he said in a surprised voice. "I actually look all right!"

"You look brilliant!" Jax told him, beaming.

Howard glanced at his watch. "I'd better go. They're expecting me home for supper."

Jax and Beans stood at the door of the café, waving him goodbye. "There's something we've forgotten," she fretted to Beans. "He's found his hidden talent. He's got a brilliant act. He's got a cool haircut so the audience can actually see his face. He's got two girl assistants and an MC. What's missing?"

Nothing, Beans told her calmly. *You've done everything you can. Now it's up to Howard.*

"Howard plus the Purr of Power," she reminded him anxiously. "You *are* coming, aren't you, Beans?"

Moonbeans blinked astonished amber-gold eyes. *Do you seriously think the Aunts would let me miss it?*

After Jax got home on the afternoon of the talent show, she and Beans popped in to check on Rumble. It was going to be a busy night and Jax knew she might not have time to go later. To her surprise, Rumble had come out of his lair. He trotted straight up to Beans and did a series of rather grumpy "brrps".

"What did he say?" Jax asked.

Beans seemed faintly embarrassed. *He says he's bored. He says he's grateful to you and your mum, but he's had enough of being cooped up and he's ready to hit the streets. He says who knows*

what the other street cats are up to without him to keep them in line?

Jax just grinned and unfastened the door. "That's okay, Beans. Tell him he can go as soon as he wants."

But it seemed that Rumble already understood. He gave Jax and Beans one last glance, before zooming out through the open door, and back into the outside world.

Jax and her mum were still smartening themselves up to go to the talent show, when the doorbell buzzed downstairs. Mum ran to the intercom to see who it was and dropped her hairbrush in amazement. "*Dad?*"

She turned to Jax, wide-eyed. "I can't believe he actually *came!*" she hissed. "What did you *say* to him, Ellie Mae?"

"I just told him he had the most hilarious laugh ever and we needed him in our audience," Jax said, grinning, and she rushed to let him in.

As soon as she saw her grandpa standing on the doorstep she flung her arms around him. "I've really missed you, Grandpa, and so has Mum!"

Grandpa did his usual grumpy snort, but she knew he was pleased, because, after she'd finished hugging him, he gave her back a loving little pat.

Later, Jax and her family walked up to the school with all the other kids and parents. "I can't imagine why you had to lug your school

136

bag to the talent show, Ellie Mae," Mum
complained.

"Maybe she's brought
her homework?"
Grandpa joked.

Jax had to hide her
grin. *No, just my magic
moon cat.*

Once they were settled in their seats,
she stealthily unfastened her bag and let an
invisible Moonbeans out into the hall.

The first part of the show was a blur. Jax was
so nervous waiting for Howard to come on that
she felt a tiny bit sick. She only really started
paying attention when Conrad came
somersaulting onto the stage at the beginning
of his street dance.

He finished his act to loud applause,
spinning around on his head like a human

spinning top. Ruby-Rose was next, reciting a comical poem about a cat that was really a spy. Being Ruby-Rose, she did it brilliantly. She had to do it in front of the curtain though, so that Saskia and Tabitha had time to get seated with their instruments.

When the curtains drew back, Jax was surprised to see Saskia looking a weird shade of green. Her hands shook as she placed her violin under her chin. For a moment, Jax thought she was going to burst into tears. Then Saskia seemed to get a grip on her nerves and she started to play the sad, dreamy melody Jax had heard coming from their house. Soon Saskia and Tabitha were bowing and smiling as the audience applauded.

"Howard's on next, Grandpa," Jax hissed as the curtain came down. "If you can't manage the big belly laugh, do your little squeaky

Gramps chuckles. I'm totally relying on you, okay?"

He patted her hand. "I'll give it my best shot, Ellie Mae."

Conrad ran on in his flash waistcoat and MC's hat. "Now I want you to raise the roof for the SPECTACULAR, SPELLBINDING, SUPER-TALENTED...MISTER MAGICK!" he bawled at the top of his voice.

Once more the curtains drew back, revealing a table covered with the props of a stage magician, including Mister Magick's top hat. Lilia and Ruby-Rose skipped on in their sparkly outfits. Howard followed, looking panicky. "I can't find Hubble!" he told them. "I can't go on! I can't do my act without Hubble."

Jax felt her mum go tense. "He's meant to say that," Jax reassured her in a whisper. "It's part of his act!"

Ruby-Rose smilingly presented Howard with the top hat. "He's in here!"

Howard looked appalled. "*Please* tell me you didn't!" He closed his eyes. "I'll never hear the end of this. Hubble is going to be so livid," he moaned. Amazed "aah"s came from the audience as he carefully lifted his rabbit out of the hat and set him down on the table on his piece of blanket.

"I am so sorry, it was an innocent mistake, okay," he told Hubble. "They didn't mean to insult you, did you, girls?" Ruby-Rose and Lilia quickly shook their heads. "They've never been a magician's assistants before. They had no idea what kind of rabbit they were dealing with."

Hubble just stared straight ahead, whiffling his nose.

"He's sulking," Howard confided in the audience. "He's been in a mood ever since he found out he couldn't have his own dressing room!"

Jax heard a few people chuckle.

"You should have heard him rant," Howard said gloomily. "He was like, 'I'm the brains behind this act, Howard. Without me there *is* no act. I think I at least deserve a dressing room and I'm sorry, but your old trainers box with a bit of straw in it is *not* a dressing room.'"

Jax's mum giggled. "He's funny."

"Hubble has got a point though," Howard told the audience. "Doing a magic act was all his idea. I wanted to enter the talent show, but then Hubble reminded me that I didn't have an actual talent." He paused for the audience's "aww"s of sympathy. "No, he's right!" he told the audience. "I seriously don't have any talents. Take the time I joined the orchestra. As I didn't play any actual instruments, Miss Cooper said she'd let me have a go on the drums. I made up my mind I was going to be the best drummer our school had ever heard." Howard beamed at the audience. "Man, I LOVED hitting those drums! I loved them so much I got a bit carried away. Actually," he confessed, "I totally mashed up the drum kit. My old man had to fork out for a new one."

Jax sneaked a look at their music teacher and saw her shaking her head and laughing.

Next Howard described his attempt to sing with the school choir, cracking everyone up with his impersonation of a foghorn. While he was talking, he kept tugging anxiously at the gaudy piece of red silk that was poking out of his sleeve. "Hubble taught me this trick," he told the audience. "Sometimes it goes totally wrong though, so don't get your hopes up, okay? Anyway, to get back to my hidden talents: so I said to Hubble, 'Maybe I could do juggling?' And Hubble said, 'Dude, you couldn't even hang on to the baton in the relay race!'" Howard shook his head. "When I first got Hubble he wouldn't have dreamed of saying 'dude'. I keep telling him he watches too much TV, and he's like, 'I don't have *thumbs*, dude! How do you expect me to turn off the TV when I don't have *thumbs*?'"

Grandpa had been obediently doing his special Gramps chuckle ever since Howard came on, but now he gave a sudden shout of laughter. At the same moment, Jax heard a booming Father Christmassy laugh from the other side of the hall. It was Howard's dad! Howard must have heard it too because he hesitated. Jax went cold inside. *He's forgotten his lines*, she panicked. Then she puffed out her cheeks with relief as Howard smoothly carried on.

"So I said, 'Well, how about acrobatics?' Hubble said, 'No way, dude. You're so uncoordinated you're dangerous! Remember when you did the long jump and landed on that wasp?' I said, 'Hubble, anyone can have an accident. No need to make a big deal out of it,' and Hubble said, 'It was a pretty big deal for that poor little wasp!'" And Howard mimed a wasp being squashed flat by his bottom.

Jax looked around the hall and saw everyone crying with laughter, even Mr. Tattersall, their headmaster.

"Then Hubble says, 'Look, dude, why don't I

help you out? I haven't told you this, but before I came to live with you I used to be in a famous magic act. I'll teach you some tricks and we'll do a double act. With my brains and talent, even if you're a rubbish magician I can make you look good.'" Howard was still tugging at the scarves all the time he was talking. He gave one final desperate tug, then looked comically dismayed as they suddenly came streaming out of his sleeve like a never-ending rainbow.

"Okay, you can stop now!" he told them nervously. Jax giggled. That line had been her idea. But the scarves didn't stop! They kept on coming, to amazed gasps from the audience, until Howard was standing in a sea of brightly coloured silk. He peered up his sleeve. "Anything else up here? Oh, hold up!" With a surprised expression, he pulled out a bunch of artificial flowers, then he peered up his other sleeve, blew out his cheeks and produced a second bunch. The audience applauded wildly as he presented the bouquets to Lilia and Ruby-Rose. He turned triumphantly to Hubble. "Ha! Not such a rubbish magician now, am I?"

With one of his snowy paws, Hubble pulled down one of his enormous droopy ears and started washing with a bored expression. Everyone roared with surprised laughter, including Jax. *That must have been Beans's idea!* she thought.

But Howard was on a roll now and he didn't even blink. "Now *that*, ladies and gentlemen, is a rabbit with attitude!" he told the audience, grinning. "I'm just grateful I've got thumbs,

otherwise it would be him pulling *me* out
of a top hat!" Howard picked up his magician's
wand and tapped the hat, the signal for
Hubble to jump back in.

"Thank you, you've been a great audience,"
Howard said, bowing, and he ran off with
Hubble, quickly followed by Ruby-Rose and
Lilia, to a storm of applause.

Before the show, Mum and Nadia had set
up a refreshments table at the
back of the hall with
special goodies from
the café. Grandpa had
offered to help, which left
Jax free to go backstage to
find Howard. But she couldn't get near him.
Too many people were crowding round to
congratulate him. Jax didn't mind.
She was just glad for Howard, and she was

totally thrilled for her and Beans. The shyest boy in Goose Green had done a stand-up routine in front of the whole school! Their mission was a brilliant success!

"That boy's got wonderful comic timing," Grandpa said on the way home. "He could be famous one day."

Jax didn't think the Aunts were too bothered about someone being famous. They just wanted everyone to be happy, and making people laugh made Howard happy.

Grandpa was happy too, Jax noticed. She heard him telling her mum he hadn't laughed so much for years. He even stayed for a cup of tea before he had to catch his bus. As he was leaving, Mum cautiously asked if he'd come over one day to help her put up some shelves.

Grandpa looked thoughtful. "I'm busy this weekend," he said after a pause. "I could come next Sunday though, if that would suit you, Laura?"

He didn't know you needed him, Beans said, when he and Jax were alone in her room.

"That's silly," Jax objected. "We always needed him."

Sometimes people need to be told, said Beans.

"I suppose," Jax said dreamily. She was looking across to see if Howard was in his room, but his window was totally dark. He was probably downstairs celebrating with his family.

Jax and her family had followed Howard and his family as they walked back from the talent show. She'd been too far away to hear what they said, but she'd noticed that Freya and Flossie had insisted on holding his hands all the way home. Jax had felt a tiny glow inside her heart, because Howard wasn't invisible any more.

She turned to smile at Beans. "You did *loads* of purring for Howard! The hall was jumping with moon vibes."

Moonbeans gave an enormous yawn, making his whiskers vibrate. *I purred for all the acts,* he explained. *I thought I should be completely fair.*

Jax climbed into bed, sleepily cuddling up to her little moon cat. She had a sudden thought. "Beans, did you do an extra purr for Saskia? You did, didn't you? That's how she got over her nerves so fast!"

But Beans just did a very loud snore. Worn out by so much purring, he was already fast asleep.

Jax was half asleep herself when for no reason she found herself remembering Howard squashing the wasp. She started shaking with laughter. "'It was a big deal for the wasp!'" she gasped. "Oh, the poor, *poor* little wasp!"

As she rolled around her bed in silent hysterics, she suddenly pictured the Aunts looking down on the exhausted moon kitten and the giggling human girl, and she had the strangest feeling that they were laughing too.

A message from Annie

Dear Readers,

Like Ellie Mae Jackson I lived just with my mum. She didn't run a café that sold magical cupcakes, she went out to work as a secretary, and in the holidays I took care of myself most days. I was often lonely and longed for a pet.

One day, most unusually, my mum took a day off from her job and even more unusually she walked me to my village school. She said she had arranged to meet one of my teachers but didn't explain why. Unlike most country people in those days, this teacher owned a car. We waited patiently outside the school gates and eventually saw him driving very carefully along the road. He stopped in front of us and I was amazed to see a tiny but extremely confident tabby kitten riding in the passenger seat. I was even more amazed when my mum explained that this kitten was for me!

I called him Tinker and he was the next best thing to a magical moon cat. He adored me from the start and when he grew older often tried to follow me to school. He seemed to know what time I'd be coming home and was always waiting for me on the corner. I shared all my thoughts and worries with Tinker, just like Jax does with Moonbeans, and I was absolutely convinced that he understood everything I was telling him. Like Moonbeans, Tinker often had to go out roaming on private cat business. Then, during the night he would jump in through my bedroom window, smelling of earth and wild flowers, and curl up with me until morning. I have known dozens of wonderful cats and kittens since then but none of them have been quite as magical and special as Tinker...except Beans. I hope you'll love my magical moon cat as much as I do. As a special treat, we've added a sneak preview of the next book – ENJOY!

Love and moon dust,
Annie xxx

www.anniedaltonwriter.co.uk

Calling all Magical Moon Cat Fans!

Read on for a sneak preview of Jax and Beans's next mission,

MOONBEANS AND THE CIRCUS OF WISHES

But remember –
it's TOP SECRET!

"What's your best thing so far?" Jax asked her friend Howard.

Jax and her friends were in the visitors' café at the Goose Green City Farm, hungrily munching burgers and chips. Outside it was a sunny but wildly windy day, which Jax thought was completely perfect weather for a class trip. As she watched, an autumn leaf flattened itself against the window of the café, then went whirling away across the farmyard.

Howard was still thinking about his best thing. "Probably the sheepdogs," he said at last. "They were cool."

"They were my best too," said Lilia, who liked to agree with people. "And the cute little lambs."

"Their jaws were like nutcrackers though!" Conrad said with a grin. "Mine almost pulled the feeding bottle right out of my hand!"

As usual, Conrad's voice was twice as loud as anyone else's in the café and their teacher gave him a sharp look. Conrad was the cheekiest boy in the school. He even *looked* cheeky, with his spiky ginger hair sticking up above his friendly freckled face. These days he was one of Jax's best friends, though it hadn't always been that way.

Watching Conrad and the others chatting

enthusiastically about their morning at the City Farm, Jax felt a twinge of sadness go through her. *I wish Moonbeans was here*, she thought. She hadn't brought him because she knew that taking a magical moon kitten on a class trip – even if he faithfully promised to stay invisible – was just asking for trouble.

Some of Moonbeans's magic must have rubbed off on her though, because the City Farm cat had been following Jax around all morning! He was called Bandit and he had a piratical black patch over one eye, and had absolutely refused to let Jax out of his sight.

"I think he can smell my cat, Beans," Jax had explained shyly to the City Farm helpers, Simon and Nan. *Can he smell that Beans is from a totally different world though*, she'd wondered. Jax was the only human in Goose Green who knew Moonbeans was from a magical alien planet, but animals always seemed to guess straight away.

At this moment, Bandit was outside the café, mewing and trying to get in every time a visitor opened the door. "Are you sure you haven't got magical powers?" Nan asked Jax, laughing as she firmly closed the door on him.

Jax nervously laughed back, but she was thinking that magic sometimes made life *really* complicated.

A rude noise surprised her out of her thoughts, but it was only Conrad, squirting extra ketchup on his burger from an almost empty plastic bottle. This earned him another sharp look from their teacher, but Conrad didn't seem to notice.

"This farm is *ace!*" he said enthusiastically. "I didn't really believe anyone could squeeze an actual farm inside a busy city, did you?"

"Not unless it was like a little *dollies'* farm!"
Ruby-Rose giggled, twirling one of her curly
bunches. Though she had completely stopped
being a child star these days, Ruby-Rose still
went in for child-star hairstyles. Today her
bunches were tied up with shiny yellow
ribbons that were pulled so tight, Jax was sure
it must be giving her a headache!

"I really loved those sheepdogs," Conrad
said wistfully. "I wish I could have a dog – or
any kind of animal really."

"Isn't it your birthday soon?" Jax said. "You
could ask your mum and dad for a puppy."

His face lit up. "I might do that." Then his
eyes clouded again. "But they'll probably say
no!"

"Why would they say no?" asked Howard.

"His little brother's got allergies," explained
Ruby-Rose.

Conrad looked dejected for a moment, then he noticed Ruby-Rose putting down her knife and fork. "Don't you want those chips, Ruby?" he asked hopefully.

"No, you can have them if you want." She pushed her plate over.

"My mum calls me the human dustbin!" Conrad was already squirting on more ketchup.

"Your mum's got a point," Lilia agreed, giggling.

After lunch, Jax's class went back out into the farmyard, where Nan and Simon were waiting. The helpers both wore faded jeans, muddy boots, and sweatshirts that said *Goose Green City Farm*. Neither of them looked anything like the country farmers Jax had seen on TV. Simon had long dreadlocks and Nan had pink spiked hair and a stud in her nose.

"We've got a surprise for you," Nan said with a grin.

When the children saw the huge horses harnessed to two old-fashioned carts, their eyes grew wide.

"They're shire horses," Simon explained. "In the old days they did the work that was too heavy for smaller horses, pulling ploughs or heavy loads. See those huge, fluffy feet? Like they're wearing ankle boots? All shire horses have those."

The nearest horse nosed hopefully at Conrad's school blazer.

"This is Punch." Nan produced a windfall apple from her pocket. "You can give this to him if you want – just keep your hand completely flat."

"Conrad, *don't!*" Lilia gasped. "His teeth are like *railings!*"

Conrad shook his head. "Punch won't hurt me." He held out Nan's apple on the flat of his hand. With incredible gentleness, the horse took it, then began to crunch with its supersized teeth.

"You're good with animals," Nan said. "Punch trusts you."

Conrad went bright red but Jax knew he was pleased...

Conrad longs to have a pet of his own, but his little brother is allergic. With Beans working on his own top secret plan, could this be Jax's toughest mission yet? Find out in...

Moonbeans and the Circus of Wishes

More deliciously delectable recipes
★ from THE DREAM CAFÉ ★

Summer has come to Goose Green!
What better way to enjoy it than with an ice-cold
glass of pink lemonade and these scrumptious treats?

 ## Strawberry Shortcakes

A cool twist on a classic scone, these sunshiney
snacks are Howard's favourite!

FOR THE SHORTCAKES (makes 10)

You will need:

225g (8oz) self-raising flour

1 teaspoon of baking powder

50g (2oz) butter

25g (1oz) caster sugar

½ teaspoon of vanilla essence

1 medium egg

5 tablespoons of milk (and extra for brushing)

FOR THE FILLING

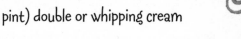

You will need:

225g (8oz) strawberries

150ml (¼ pint) double or whipping cream

You will also need a round cutter about 6cm (2½in) across.

1. Heat the oven to 220°C / Gas mark 7. Use a paper towel to wipe a little butter over a baking tray.

2. Sift the flour and baking powder into a big bowl. Cut the butter into chunks. Stir them into the flour.

3. Use the tips of your fingers and thumbs to pick up some butter and flour, and squash and rub them together. Carry on doing this.

4. The lumps of butter will gradually get smaller and smaller. Keep on rubbing until they are the size of small breadcrumbs. Then, stir in the sugar.

5. Break the egg into a cup. Add the milk and vanilla. Mix with a fork, then pour into the big bowl.

6. Use a blunt knife to cut through the mixture again and again, to mix it. It will cling together. Pat it into a ball with your hands.

7. Dust a clean work surface with flour. Put the dough on the flour. Roll over the dough, turn it around and roll over it again, until it's 1cm (½in) thick.

8. Cut out lots of rounds. Put them on the tray. Squash the scraps together, roll them out again and cut more rounds.

9. Brush a little milk onto each round. Bake for 10-12 minutes, until risen and golden brown. Move to a wire rack, to cool.

10. Remove the green stalk from the strawberries. Cut the strawberries into thin slices.

11. Whip the cream. To do this, pour the cream into a large bowl. Hold the bowl firmly. Beat the cream with a whisk as quickly as you can, until the cream becomes stiff. When you lift the whisk, the cream should stand up in a floppy point. Be careful you don't beat the cream too much, or the cream will go hard – yuck!

12. Cut each shortcake in half. Spread some cream on each lower half. Top with strawberry slices. Spread on more cream. Put the top halves back on and sift a little icing sugar over the top of the finished shortcakes. Yumm!

* Only fill as many shortcakes as you want to eat! You can store the rest for later.

* Why not replace the strawberries with raspberries, blackberries or blueberries?

Butterfly Cakes

These gorgeous mini cakes are spread with a creamy chocolate topping called ganache, and the top of the cake is used to make wings shaped like a butterfly's – they're one of Beans's favourite treats.
But sssh…don't tell Mum!

FOR THE CAKES (makes about 25)

You will need:

40g (1½oz) caster suar

40g (1½oz) soft margarine

40g (1½oz) self-raising flour

1 medium egg

1½ teaspoons of cocoa powder

FOR THE PLAIN OR MILK CHOCOLATE GANACHE

You will need:

40g (1½oz) plain or milk chocolate

2 tablespoons of double cream

FOR THE WHITE CHOCOLATE GANACHE

You will need:

60g (2½oz) white chocolate

2 tablespoons of double cream

You will also need 25 mini paper cake cases.
PLUS! Chocolate beans, sugar sprinkles and chocolate
writing icing to decorate

1. Heat the oven to 180°C / Gas mark 4. Arrange
the paper cases on a baking tray.

2. Put the sugar and margarine
in a big bowl. Sift the flour.
Break the egg into a cup, then
pour it in. Mix it all together.

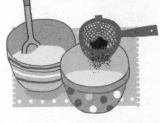

3. Spoon half the mixture into
another bowl. Sift the cocoa
powder over it. Mix it in.

4. Spoon the chocolate mixture
into half the paper cases, and
the vanilla mixture into the rest
of the cases. Bake for 10-12
minutes, or until risen and firm.

5. Leave for a few minutes, then put on a wire rack to cool. Meanwhile, make the chocolate ganache – yum!

6. First melt the chocolate. Start by putting it in a heatproof bowl. Fill a pan a quarter full of water and put it over a medium heat. Carefully lower the bowl into the pan, leave for 5 minutes, then stir the chocolate until it is melted. Now stir in the cream, and lift the bowl out of the pan. Let the mixture cool for 10 minutes before putting it in the fridge for 1 hour, stirring every now and then. No nibbles allowed!

7. When the cakes are cold, take them out of their cases. Slice the top off each cake. Then, cut each top into 2 semicircles.

8. Spread some ganache on the top of each cake. Gently push 2 semicircles into the ganache on each cake, to make wings.

9. You could make a head from a chocolate bean and pipe on dots of chocolate writing icing for eyes. Scatter on some sugar sprinkles to decorate the butterfly's body.

Pineapple Cake ✿

Tuck in to this tangy, tropical party cake made using canned crushed pineapple. Filled and topped with cream cheese frosting, it's really refreshing on hot summer afternoons.

FOR THE CAKE (serves 12)
You will need:
250g (9oz) plain flour
2 teaspoons of baking powder
125g (4½oz) soft dark brown sugar
2 teaspoons of ground cinnamon
150ml (¼pint) sunflower or vegetable oil
3 large eggs
1 teaspoon of vanilla essence
400g (14oz) can of crushed pineapple

FOR THE CREAM CHEESE FROSTING
You will need:
400g (14oz) full-fat cream cheese, at room temperature
150g (5oz) icing sugar

You will also need 2 x 20cm (8in) round, shallow cake
tins, and dried pineapple pieces, to decorate.

1. Heat the oven to 180°C/ Gas mark 4. Put the cake
tins on some baking parchment and draw around them.
Then cut out the shape, cutting just inside the line. Wipe
a little softened butter or cooking oil over the inside of the
tin, using a paper towel. Put the parchment shape in the
bottom of the tin.

2. Put the flour, baking powder,
sugar and cinnamon in a large bowl.
Mix. Put the oil in another bowl.
Break each egg into a cup. Add it
to the oil, with the vanilla, beating
the oil mixture with a fork.

3. Put 2 tablespoons of
pineapple in a small bowl.
Add the rest to the oil and
egg mixture. Stir it in.

4. Mix the oil mixture into the
flour mixture. Divide between the
cake tins. Bake for 25 minutes,
until risen and golden brown.

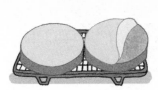

5. Leave the cakes in their tins for 10 minutes. Then, turn them out on a wire rack. Peel off the baking parchment and leave the cakes to cool completely.

6. Now it's time to make the cream cheese frosting. Sift the icing sugar into a large bowl and add the cream cheese. Mix gently, along with the pineapple you set aside earlier.

7. When the cakes are cold, put one on a plate, flat side down. Spread over half the frosting. Put the other cake on top, flat side down. Spread on the remaining frosting. Arrange the dried pineapple pieces on top of the frosting to decorate.

ARE YOU NUTS FOR NUTS?

Why not follow steps 1-3, then add 50g (2oz) of pecan or walnut pieces to the oil mixture. Follow steps 4-7, then decorate the top of your cake with yummy pecan or walnut pieces.

You can find all these YUMMY recipes,
plus LOADS more in

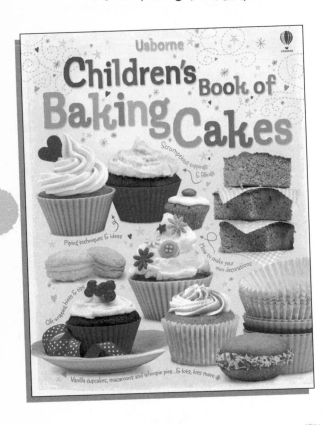

OUT NOW!

ISBN: 9781409523369

Fancy finding out some dreamy cake
decorating tips?

Or are you a creative kitten in need
of a Magical Moon Cat
colouring sheet?

BLAST OFF to
www.magicalmooncat.com

Jax and Beans are waiting!

My Magical Moon Cat Page

Hey there! It's me, Jax. Has reading about Howard made you determined to discover YOUR hidden talent? I hope so!

Are you a creative cook? Note down your secret ingredients here.

Jazz up this page with your Moonbeans stickers!

What's YOUR next mission?
Keep track here!

Doodle, draw,
plan or plot –
anything goes!

Magical Moon Cat

Join Jax and Moonbeans and collect every magical mission!

Moonbeans and the Dream Café
When Jax and her mum move house to follow Mum's dream of opening a cool café, Jax feels fed up and lonely. But then a sparkly pink lightning bolt delivers a cute alien kitten to Jax's home, and it looks like her luck is about to change!
ISBN: 9781409526315

Moonbeans and the Shining Star
When Moonbeans announces he's on a mission to cheer up stroppy starlet, Ruby-Rose, Jax is dismayed. Ruby-Rose thinks she's the bee's knees because she goes to stage school. But is it just an act?

ISBN: 9781409526322

Moonbeans and the Circus of Wishes
Beans's wish to find his Earth-cat dad looks set to come true, after Jax and Beans discover he's living with a travelling circus. But Jax is worried. Could this spell the end of their adventures together?
ISBN: 9781409526346

For more amazing adventures, zoom to
www.fiction.usborne.com